A Babysitter's Guide to

MONSTER HUNTING 2

BEASTS & GEEKS

JOE BALLARINI

ILLUSTRATED BY VIVIENNE TO

KATHERINE TEGEN BOOKS
An Imprint of HarperCollins Publishers

ALSO BY JOE BALLARINI

A Babysitter's Guide to Monster Hunting

Katherine Tegen Books is an imprint of HarperCollins Publishers.

A Babysitter's Guide to Monster Hunting #2: Beasts & Geeks
Text copyright © 2018 by Joe Ballarini
Illustrations copyright © 2018 by Vivienne To
All rights reserved. Printed in the United States of America.
No part of this book may be used or reproduced in any manner whatsoever without written permission except in the case of brief quotations embodied in critical articles and reviews. For information address HarperCollins Children's Books, a division of HarperCollins Publishers, 195 Broadway, New York, NY 10007.
www.harpercollinschildrens.com

Library of Congress Control Number: 2017954124
ISBN 978-0-06-243787-7

Typography by Joel Tippie
18 19 20 21 22   CG/LSCH   10 9 8 7 6 5 4 3 2 1
❖
First Edition

For Theo, my favorite monster,
and for every kid who has ever felt
like a lost, hairy mutant

Behind me, a massive, fifteen-foot-long worm the size of a Winnebago snaked its way through the trees with frightening speed. Trees snapped under its weight.

My book bag bobbled on my back as I ran ignoring the cold wind biting my cheeks.

Snerff-snerff, grunted the creature's slimy snout at my sneaker heels.

Two things about me: I'm a Libra and I hate bugs. The smallest cockroach can send me screaming out of the room. It's not something I'm proud of, but I can't help it. Their skinny limbs and greasy shells send me to Willy City.

Up ahead I could see a break in the trees. Finally, a little moonlight.

Freedom. Safety. *Sweet.*

Actually, it was a rocky gorge overlooking a rushing river.

Doom. Death. *Darn.*

I barely had time to stop. Pebbles scattered over the edge, plunking into the churning rapids a hundred feet below. With nowhere else to go, I scrambled up a tree trunk. Perched on a branch, I opened my red spiral-bound notebook.

From Kelly Ferguson's copy of
A Babysitter's Guide to Monster Hunting:

NAME: Night crawler
TYPE: Lumbricus terrestris disgustus
LIKES: Flesh and bones
SKILLS: Digesting humans in its belly for a period of six months
WEAKNESSES: Sunlight. Great white sharks.

I slapped the guide shut. "Whose weakness *isn't* great white sharks?"

Balancing on a branch, I saw the huge, plump night crawler wind its way up toward me.

It can climb trees? That's not in the guide!

Long snout-feelers wrapped around the tree limb I was standing on and drew me toward its widening mouth and tiny jagged teeth. I scrambled up to the very peak of the tree. The mist-blanketed forest swept out in every direction. I let out a futile scream, even though I knew no one was close enough to hear me. The only things in my backpack were the guide, a bag of almonds, a compass, a map of the woods, and a flashlight. No weapons. No hardware. All part of tonight's test.

"So, Kelly, how was your weekend?" I said. "Oh, fine. Y'know, got chased through the woods by a night crawler in the hopes of passing my babysitter training exam, but I failed miserably, and now I'm going to be slowly digested in its stomach for the next six months. You?"

The branches shook and the tree began to tilt. The weight of the killer worm was pulling the evergreen down over the edge of the cliff.

Roots tore from the ground, and we went horizontal. Bark peeled under my fingernails. The night crawler squealed and slipped, dangling by its creepy feelers as its tail thrashed above the churning, rocky river.

I wrapped my legs tightly around the branch. One wrong tremor would break the last tree root, sending me and the oversized earthworm falling to our deaths.

If a girl falls to her doom in the woods and no one is around to hear her scream, does she make a sound? Answer: yes. And that sound is "Aaaaaaah— SPLAT!"

My shaking hands grabbed the branch above me. I climbed the almost-upside-down tree. Fleshy feelers lashed at me until—

Snap! The final root broke.

Everything went weightless. I scaled up the rest of the tree and launched myself into the air, both hands desperately reaching for the faraway, grassy ledge. I caught a single broken root and held on. The shrill cry of the night crawler rang out as it plummeted into the rapids. Imagine dropping a water balloon off your roof. Now imagine that water balloon was filled with seven hundred pounds of yellow slime and chunks of mystery meat.

I shuddered. Bugs are just *ew*.

I climbed to safety, wiped the dirt off my jeans, and picked bits of pine needles and bark off my face. Sticky sap stuck to my hair in clumps, giving me that fresh-and-feral look.

"Knew I should've brought my hair band," I grumbled.

The clinking of bells in the sky made me look up, and I saw a small glowing orb.

Recon pixie.

"I'm cool, Penelope!" I said, waving up at her. "Thanks for asking. If that *is* what you were asking."

The ball of firelight chimed.

"I don't speak Pixie. I was just kind of saying hi."

Ting-a-ting!

"Again, no clue what you're saying."

Penelope flew off, trailing glittery sparkles while I tripped over a branch and ate dirt.

"Good talk, Penelope," I said.

A couple of months ago I was completely oblivious to this unseen world of horrors and wonders. I was happy being miserable in middle school. Just a normal kid. Technically, I'm still just a kid. Thirteen years old. The normal part is highly questionable.

I started babysitting because I wanted to pay for summer camp. Beautiful, sweet Camp Miskatonic. I had no idea I would be joining an ancient secret society of monster hunters sworn to protect kids (and the rest of world) from the forces of evil.

Now, in a cruel twist of fate, I was in a bleak, cold, two-day, dead-of-winter camp, where the daily activities were weapons training, tackling obstacle courses, running for your life from man-eating creatures, bunking with strange kids, and questioning all my life choices.

The weekend was sort of like the infamous two weeks in H-E Double Hockey Sticks that the Navy SEALs go through—only ours was jammed into one weekend, because, unlike Navy SEALs, we all have to go back to school on Monday and pretend like none of this ever happened. I'd like to see a Navy SEAL finish their training and then ace a book report on S. E. Hinton's *The Outsiders*.

All around the world, from the Midwest to Mongolia, each babysitter chapter was holding their annual training exam to see who had the chops to become a babysitter. Fighting monsters is a global effort.

Tonight's fun-filled horror show was a competition to see who could escape a monster attack in the shortest amount of time. Earlier in the evening, I willingly gave my scent to an instructor, who gave it to the night crawler so that the lard bag would chase me through the cursed woods. The less time it took me to outrun it, the more points I would score. The more points I scored, the closer I would be to becoming an official member of the Rhode Island chapter of the Order of the Babysitters.

Was I insane for enjoying all of this? Obvs. It sounds supes cheese, but I took pride in my duty to protect kids from the creatures of the night.

And no, I hadn't yet told my mom and dad what I *really* did when I went out babysitting. They just thought I was a dorky go-getter. I mean, I'd tell them one day—far, far, far in the future when they couldn't ground me for life. But for the moment, I just wanted to get through Heck Weekend in one piece.

A mound of boulders formed a strange, lopsided skull-like face in the moonlight. A rusty, yellow "Danger: Falling Rocks" sign jutted from its side.

I grabbed the tooth of the huge skull-like rock and twisted it three times to the left and once to the right. There was a muffled sound of gears and grinding stone as the mound slowly rolled apart, revealing a ramshackle, two-floor, ivy-covered cottage. Colored Christmas lights were draped in the windows, and a giant wreath hung on the front door. At the very peak of the Victorian-era roof, beside a jumble of high-tech antennae and satellite dishes, there was a flag with the babysitter's crest.

A highly secured monster stable, with locks and chains on each of the doors, stretched alongside the cabin. Cages rattled, bucked by howling creatures inside. The rocks tumbled back into place behind me, hiding the small fortress known to only a select few as the Rhode Island headquarters for the Order of the Babysitters.

The more time I spent at the cottage, the more it felt like home.

"Fifty-shixsh minutesh and sheventeen sheconds!" Cassie McCoy lisped through her elaborate braces, clicking a stopwatch in my face.

Of course Cassie had volunteered to be the weekend's timekeeper.

"Nice to see you, too, Cassie," I said. "Am I the first one back?"

"Not by a long shot, shishter," she said, scribbling down my time on her clipboard.

"Is fifty-six minutes bad?" I asked.

"Madame Moon and Mama Vee want everyone to wait in the mesh hall," Cassie said, walking away.

All I wanted to do was slump on the couch, warm

my tootsies by the fire, and relax under the three-headed skeleton of a sea serpent.

"Is that a good time or what?" I asked.

Cassie had been in a huff all weekend because Curtis Critter, the kooky boy in our RI babysitter squad, was a no-show. Cassie had a raging, not-so-secretive crush on him. I knew this because whenever Cassie was in the same room with Curtis, a long line of drool would spill down her chin and onto her shirt. She'd bark orders at him like "Come sit by me!" or "Accept my friend request!" I guess she took his absence as a sign that he didn't feel the same way about her.

"That's a great time, Kelly," said Berna Vincent.

Berna's pink unicorn pajamas and fluffy bunny slippers made me smile. She handed me a steaming cup of something cinnamony and delicious.

Berna rocks. Ever since Halloween, we've been hanging out a lot. Turns out fighting an army of nightmares together is a great bonding experience for a blossoming friendship. But Berna and I are more than just allies against evil. I really like her. She never makes me feel dumb, even though she is a walking Wiki.

In the mess hall, four worn-out, wannabe babysitters from around New England sat at a long wooden table. Like me, they came here in the hopes of passing the entrance exam to get into their state's babysitter

11

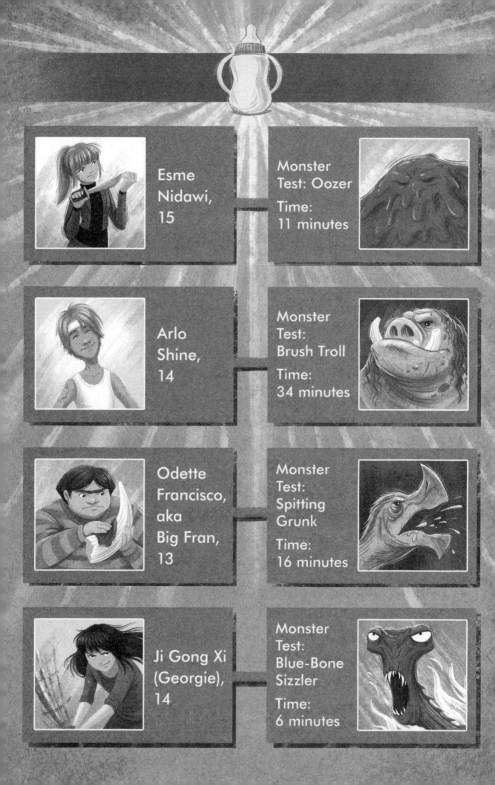

chapters. And like me, they looked like they had been chased, bitten, and hunted by monsters all night.

My shoulders drooped. It had taken me fifty-six minutes to outrun a stupid worm, and these guys aced their monsters in less time than it takes me to burn microwave popcorn. I bit the inside of my cheek. I had a sudden need to speak with the toughest, coolest baby-sitter around: my associate and mentor.

"I'm gonna go find Liz."

"Vee and Madame Moon shaid to wait in the mesh hall!" Cassie scolded as I walked up the creaky stair-case. "Don't come crying to me when they dock you pointsh for being abshent!"

I walked down the second-floor hallway to a door covered in a decoupage of punk rock heroes, evil eyes, and a spray-painted sign:

DANGER
keep Out
seriously,
that Means You

I knocked, got no answer, and slowly opened the door. A shock-top of spiky hair, half of which had been recently dyed electric pink, bobbed behind a mound of books. Liz LeRue was sitting cross-legged on the floor, headphones blasting, furiously scanning a book about—*shudder*—giant spiders.

"Any luck?" I said, leaning down.

Liz spun, tackled me, and held her ballpoint pen above my eyeball.

"Dude!" I screamed. "It's me! Kelly! K-Ferg!"

Liz lowered her pen and returned to hunching over her book. "Don't sneak up on me."

Plates of uneaten, rotten food were strewn all over the floor beside dozens of crushed Monster Energy drinks and cold mugs of coffee. Maps dotted with pins and crisscrossed with red strings hung on the walls.

"Maybe it's time you take a break," I suggested. "Or a shower."

Liz flicked a page. For the past month Liz had grown obsessed with the Grand Guignol's final words to us: *Don't ask me, darling. Ask Serena.*

The Grand Guignol was the narcissistic, goat-legged Boogeyman we defeated on Halloween (see guide entry #665). That monster took Liz's little brother, Kevin, eight years ago. Little Kevin's disappearance shattered Liz's family and ruined her entire life. She confided in me that she became a babysitter as an act of vengeance, but I also knew that underneath her tough, black-leather-jacket-and-army-boot exterior, there was a soft, sad girl's heart, clinging to the hope she would one day find her little brother and fix her broken family.

Ask Serena.

Like a cryptic tweet from a crazy dictator, that single sentence sent Liz spiraling.

Serena was one of the seven deadly Boogeypeople. Sidenote: since three of them are female, I prefer the term "Boogey*people*." It doesn't have the same ring as Boogeymen, but I don't care. I believe in equality even when it comes to monsters.

No matter how much we Googled Serena, nothing came up except a bunch of pictures of spiders. Word of advice: never Google spiders.

When we called the London Council of Babysitters for help, the only information they could provide was a portrait of Serena painted in 1793, when she married the Earl of Wanstead. The London office shipped the portrait to the Rhode Island chapter, saying that they were happy to be rid of it. When we opened the wooden crate that held the portrait, we found out why.

Her eyes radiated an icy darkness that made me feel like I was listening to the saddest angst-ridden folk song while standing in the rain, staring at homeless kittens huddled in a soggy cardboard box. Basically, alone, hopeless, and like nothing I could ever do would make a difference. I threw the painting in the basement and haven't looked at it since.

"Find anything else on her?" I asked.

"Check the guide," Liz said.

From Liz LeRue's copy of
A Babysitter's Guide to Monster Hunting:

NAME: Serena von Kessell, aka the Spider Queen, aka Red Widow, aka Princess Tarantula, aka Serena Salazar
TYPE: Half spider, half human
LIKES: Blood of all kinds. The younger the better.

STRENGTHS: The most beautiful and charming of all seven Boogies (great fashion sense). Her fangs eject a deadly venom that can bewitch, paralyze, or kill her prey, depending on her mood.

WEAPONS: A powerful, sticky web shoots from a gland above her butt, just like a spider.

WEAKNESSES: Jewelry. Flattery. Giant ego. Eight legs means eight feet; eight feet means more toes to step on.

Liz snapped the guide shut. "I've been following her tracks," she said. "In 1793 she married the Earl of Wanstead. This guy."

She fished around the scattered books and held up one opened to an entry on the Earl of Wanstead.

"Doesn't look like a monster to me," I said.

"He wasn't. He was just a lonely dude related to the British monarchy, and also stinking rich," she said. "He died mysteriously three months later. Broke and penniless. My hunch is she drained him of his blood and his bank account."

"Must have been one bad honeymoon."

"Then in Paris 1849," Liz continued, "a record of a babysitter who had a brief sighting of Serena with the heir to the German Empire at an opera house. Also rich and powerful. Three months later he's pushing daisies."

"I'm sensing a pattern here," I said.

Liz held up an old, yellowed Austrian newspaper dated 1905.

"'We are pleased to announce the marriage of Duke Heinrich Schönerer and his young, captivating bride, Serena Salazar.'"

"You can read Austrian?" I asked.

"The Berlin babysitters translated it for me. One month later . . ."

"Let me guess. You found his obituary."

Liz pointed to an obituary for the dearly departed and drained duke. "He died of, get this, a lethal spider bite."

"So, she marries super rich guys, drains 'em of blood and money, and then goes underground in search of another victim."

Liz shook her head, bewildered. "And she never gets old."

"Love to know her beauty regimen."

"It's blood. Human blood."

Yuck. Why couldn't it have been a magic mud mask? Liz walked over to her wall map.

"I did a massive search for rich guys who died of spider bites or blood loss, and I was able to follow her

trail. She was in Istanbul in 1914. Germany in 1929. Israel in 1967."

I narrowed my eyes at the crimson web. "She seems to like places on the brink of war."

"Or maybe she helped drive them to it."

"You think she, like, used her powers to tip those countries over the edge?"

Liz looked at me. Dead serious. "Kelly. These are the Boogeymen we're talking about."

"Boogey*people*," I corrected. Liz rolled her eyes.

"They will do anything to destroy humanity."

Looking at the places and times Serena had visited filled my heart with the same cold and overwhelming darkness I felt when I gazed into the haunting eyes of her portrait.

"So. Where is she now?" I whispered.

On the map, Liz stretched a final red thread across the Atlantic and wrapped it around a pin stuck in New York City.

Only three hours from us.

"**K**elly! Liz!" screamed Berna from downstairs. "Come quick!"

We rushed to the lab to see Mama Vee and Madame Moon laying the last of the babysitter contenders on the bed. Enzo Calabrazzi, a short class clown from Boston, was unconscious, and his face was smeared with a sticky, blackish-purple sludge.

Penelope, the glowing recon pixie, spun frantically over Enzo's body. Vee pulled at the ooze covering his face. The other trainees and I crowded in the doorway and watched in terror as the rubbery goo thrashed in Mama Vee's hand. It was alive and fighting back.

"It's gone down his throat," Mama Vee said. Her long platinum hair was coming unbraided.

21

"Don't touch it!" screamed Madame Moon.

"I know what I'm doing, Leanne," said Vee as she struggled with the Scumsucker.

Madame Leanne Moon, the head of the entire New England operation, had come to oversee Heck Weekend. As the head sitter, Madame Moon outranked all of us, including Mama Vee. There had been a weird tension between them the whole weekend.

"You're agitating it, and it's expanding into his windpipe," scolded Madame Moon.

The blubber stuck in Enzo's mouth wrapped itself around Vee's arm.

"It's coming loose—don't just stand there. Help me!" said Vee.

Vee scowled at Madame Moon while the creature undulated between them. "You're the one who assigned the kid a Scumsucker when I specifically told you not to."

"Ooooh!" said Big Fran, who seemed highly amused.

Madame Moon and Vee glared at us.

"Liz, get them out of here!" Vee shouted.

Liz ushered us out of the lab and closed the door in our faces.

"You heard the lady," said Cassie, trying to take charge. "Everyone upshtairsh! You're going to want to be well reshted for tomorrow. Your final tesht. And trusht me, it'sh going to be horrible."

5

The next day Big Fran, Georgie, Arlo, Esme, and I stood at attention before a rocky waterfall, deep in the hidden woods behind HQ. I hadn't spent much time back here because, despite the beautiful setting, Vee warned me there were things lurking in the lake I was not yet ready to face. Madame Moon and Mama Vee marched to the front of the misty falls.

"Welcome to your final test!" Madame Moon shouted over the rippling waves. "Unfortunately, Enzo will not be joining us. Let this be a lesson to all of you." Madame Moon stared us down. "Babysitting requires your utmost attention. It must not be taken lightly."

Little harsh.

"Now, then!" said Madame Moon, clapping her

hands together. "Your final test is in there." She pointed to the roaring waterfall behind her. "All you need to know is its name is Kang. Good luck."

"Do we get to bring a weapon?" asked Georgie.

"Not every test can be solved with fighting," said Mama Vee. "Sometimes standing your ground can be an act of defiance."

"Running for your life works too," I grumbled.

"The Mighty Kang will look into your very soul. If it deems you worthy, it will let you live."

I raised a trembling hand. "And if it doesn't?"

Madame Moon shrugged. "Swallows you whole. Who wants to go first?"

She held out a scuba mask and a wet suit. We all stood frozen, gawking bug-eyed at the cascading falls. Were they really going to send us into the jaws of a giant? I'm pretty sure someone's parents would sue over that. But then one of our parents would have to know what we were doing.

"Kelly Ferguson," said Madame Moon. "Very brave of you to volunteer to be the first one in."

I didn't volunteer. Mama Vee winked at me, as if to say, *You got this.* Vee was my sitter when I was a little kid, and she'd taken me under her wing since I'd decided to become a babysitter. I couldn't disappoint her.

I must have hesitated for too long, because Madame

Moon looked confused. "Sorry, my mistake. I thought I was talking to the Kelly Ferguson who vanquished the Grand Guignol and his army of nightmares on All Hallows Eve. Wrong Kelly?"

"That's me," I mumbled.

The other kids looked at me in shock.

"Whoa! *You're* the newbie who killed the Grand Guignol?" shouted Big Fran. "I had no idea!"

"Why didn't you tell us?" cried Arlo.

"Been kind of a busy weekend," I said.

"Kelly Ferguson," whispered Georgie, looking at me strangely.

"If I were you, I'd wear a T-shirt with my own face on it," said Big Fran.

I felt my cheeks flush red.

"Then what are you waiting for, Kelly?" said Madame Moon. "Show us how it's done."

The wet suit gave me a serious wedgie as I scrambled across the slippery rocks toward the powerful waterfall. Through the shimmering wall of water, I could see a faint, glowing light. There was a cave hiding behind the falls.

"Go get 'em!" shouted Berna from the shore. "Just think warm thoughts!"

Warm thoughts: sunshine, kittens, and not being here.

I pulled my scuba mask over my eyes, took a deep breath, and jumped.

SPLASH! I landed in a pool of icy water. Pins and needles shot through my body. The falls punched down on me, sending me spinning. My arms and legs went numb as I desperately swam toward a rock and pulled myself onto the sand.

"So cold! So cold!" I screamed.

My voice echoed. I removed my mask and watched as ripples of sunlight waved along the walls of the gigantic cavern. In the shadowy depths a dark shape breathed. I ducked behind a boulder.

Since when do boulders have a pulse?

My rocky hiding place was layered with large spikes and scales. I was crouching behind the tail of a fifty-foot-long sleeping serpent.

Classic me.

With shaking hands, I unwrapped my guide from its plastic bag and opened it to *C*.

From Kelly Ferguson's copy
of *A Babysitter's Guide to Monster Hunting*:

NAME: The Mighty Kang
HEIGHT: Twenty-three feet
AGE: Nine hundred years old!
TYPE: Class 9 Cloud Serpent

ORIGIN: Shisha Pangma Cave in the Himalayan Mountains

LIKES: Sleeping. Retirement. Eating the unworthy.

DISLIKES: The unworthy. Loud music. Being woken up or made to do anything.

STRENGTHS: Flight. Astral projection. Oracle-like dreams.

CURRENT RESIDENCE: The waterfall behind Rhode Island headquarters

NOTE: It sees in you what you can't see in you.

"The heck does that mean?" I whispered.

A low snore made me look up from the guide.

Long, ivory feathers plumed from the Mighty Kang's back. Wonderstruck, I found myself walking the length of its body, which was rhythmically rising and falling with each enormous breath. I quietly put the guide away as I approached its huge, doglike nose. Its wrinkled eyelids were closed, sleeping.

Such a beautiful creature.

The brain-freeze level of pain in my body melted away as I reached out my hand to touch its coiled horns.

I couldn't help myself. They were ringed with feathers. I ran my hands along its soft fur and pearl scales. It was warm; not scary at all. Then its long neck uncurled, and a pair of angry, yellow-and-black eyes glared down at me, and all those enchanting warm fuzzies vanished into a puddle of near pants-peeing fear.

The great serpent reared back, hovering over me with a grin that reminded me of a cat about to eat a mouse.

Be brave, Kelly, I thought. *They wouldn't send you here if they didn't think you could survive this. Or would they? Madame Moon doesn't seem to dig your chili.*

The serpent cocked its head, swaying back and forth. I didn't dare break eye contact. I couldn't. I was mesmerized. So, I engaged in the longest, craziest staring contest of my entire life.

Say something. How do I make small talk with a Cloud Serpent?

"Hey there," I said, my voice cracking. "Y-y-you must be the Mighty Kang. It is a great honor to meet a, um, Cloud Serpent."

I bowed as if I were meeting the Queen of England. This was not in the guide, but it felt like the right thing to do.

"My name's Kelly. And, uh, I'm here because Madame Moon and Mama Vee sent me? I'm not, like, here to steal your gold or anything. Not that I see any gold. Not that all serpents hoard gold. I don't mean to stereotype serpents. Nice place. You live alone?"

"Ssssilence!" it hissed in a murky voice.

"Sure, yeah, silence. I can do that," I said.

"Ugh. Jussst ssstop talking!"

I zipped my lips and threw away the key. The Mighty Kang unfurled a pair of translucent wings and let out a guttural shriek.

"Bow your head and prepare to be judged."

I lowered my head and felt the bottom of its wispy beard brush the back of my neck. My insides were a fireworks factory explosion.

Its huge wet dog-snout nudged into me, sniffing. I chanced a look up. Wrinkled, whiskery lips slowly peeled back, revealing deadly fangs. The serpent's tail coiled around me, pinning my arms, and lifted me off the ground.

Oh no! It's found me unworthy! Am I unworthy? I thought I was doing okay.

"No, please! Oh Great and Mighty Kang, I only came here because I want to do good things and help make the world a better place and I have a feeling you do too otherwise you wouldn't be here—"

I wheezed as the air was crushed out of me.

"Jussst becausssse I am in your guide doesssssn't mean you know me, child."

30

"Yeah, but let's be honest, you could live wherever you want. You don't have to spend the winter in some damp cave behind a waterfall, but I think you do it because you like living next to the babysitters. Or it means they're protecting you maybe? From other bad monsters? Which maybe makes you a good monster and not a bad one. Am I warm?"

The serpent threw back its old head and shook with a deep, unsettling laugh. Its tail relaxed, and I could breathe again.

"You are wissse. And a bit ssssilly. You have much to learn on your quesssst." The Mighty Kang leaned its furry chin on the ground. "I will let you live."

"Thank you, Oh Big and Frightening Kang," I said, bowing my head repeatedly.

"Thisssss time."

Gulp.

"Before you go I musssst warn you. Lassst night I sssaw a vision."

"A vision about me?"

"No. Your aunt Mabel." The serpent started laughing again, its golden eyes focused on me. "Yesssss. You."

Then it spoke with a chilling voice. "Protect the turtle hatchling."

I blinked. Maybe I misheard. "Turtle hatchling?" I asked.

The shimmering serpent nodded. "The turtle will bring peace to the world of sssssun and air."

"I see," I said, nodding as if I understood what the Mighty Kang was saying.

"Don't jussst agree. Lisssssssssssssten. Ugh. Per-happssss I should jussst eat you."

"No, please! I got it. Protect the turtle. I will do that. That's our job, right? Protect kids?"

Kang burst into a gleeful giggle fit. I laughed along with it, even though I was totally terrified. "Among other thingssssss."

"But seriously. I don't know any turtles—"

WHOOSH! The end of its feathery tail swung around, batting me off my feet. I crashed through the waterfall, landing with a shriek in the freezing cold lake.

"A turtle?" Mama Vee asked for the third time.

"Maybe it's code for something," Madame Moon suggested.

We were in Vee's office on the top floor of babysitter HQ. Despite the collection of daggers and monster skulls lining the walls, it was cozy and threadbare. I was glad to be sitting by a fire in warm clothes.

"Or maybe," I said, hopeful, "it was just a dream. The other night I had a dream I was at school, but I wasn't wearing any pants. We're talking total Donald Duck. I woke up and I was like *phew*."

"This is not a time for jokes," said Madame Moon, looking at a clipboard.

"Wasn't really joking," I mumbled.

Madame Moon took a big long sniff. Her eyes felt like heat lamps on my forehead.

"You barely made it through this weekend, Miss Ferguson. Aside from Enzo, you scored the lowest out of everyone here."

I cringed. I pride myself on my good grades and perfect attendance in middle school, but I had only been at this for a month.

HECK WEEKEND REPORT CARD

Kelly Ferguson

Subject	Grade
Monster run & wrangle	F –
Hand-to-claw combat	F
Diaper defense	D+
Tactical slime survival	F +
Undead anatomy	D –
Boogeymen ballistics	C
Demon demolition	F
Monster mashing	F –
Babysitter history & theory	C+

"I handled the written exam well," I said.

"Really?" said Mama Vee, peering over Madame Moon's shoulder.

"She didn't wrangle the night crawler and return it to the stable."

Mama Vee crinkled her nose. "Oh yeah. You lost a whole grade for that one."

"I was supposed to bring that big bug back here?" I said.

"We are not barbarians, young lady," said Madame Moon. "We try to study these creatures, not just throw them off cliffs."

"It was on loan from the Great Lakes chapter," said Mama Vee. "We're gonna owe them big-time."

"It was trying to kill me!" I said in my defense.

"Well, of course it was!" shot Madame Moon. "It wouldn't be any kind of a test if it wasn't, now would it?" On the wall behind her hung a minotaur's skull. It looked like the horns were coming from Madame Moon's head.

"Learning from one's failures is the only way to improve one's successes," said Mama Vee, trying to keep things calm. "So, Kelly, what did you learn?"

I blanked. I was supposed to be scribbling notes while I was running for my life? In the silence I heard a wooden creak. A shadow under the side door stepped aside. Someone was eavesdropping on our conversation, and none of the adults seemed to notice.

"Night crawlers can climb trees. I wasn't expecting that. And it certainly wasn't in the guide."

Mama Vee nodded thoughtfully.

"Add it to the guides," said Madame Moon. An eternity passed as she wrote something down on her clipboard.

"I'm deferring your graduation," Madame Moon said flatly. "You shall remain a sitter in training."

"What?" I shot to my feet.

The scratching of her pen stopped with a forceful period that felt like a judge's gavel coming down.

"You are not a babysitter."

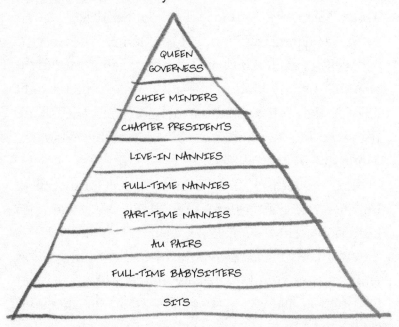

QUEEN GOVERNESS

CHIEF MINDERS

CHAPTER PRESIDENTS

LIVE-IN NANNIES

FULL-TIME NANNIES

PART-TIME NANNIES

AU PAIRS

FULL-TIME BABYSITTERS

SITS

I took a sharp breath. A sick lump filled my heart.

"Look. I can do better," I said, looking to Mama Vee for help.

"You need to do more than better!" Madame Moon slammed her fist on the desk.

"Take it easy, Leanne," said Mama Vee. "You didn't see Kelly on Halloween. She was a champ. She's only been at this a month. Those other sitters have been training for a year. I think Kelly's doing her best."

Madame Moon shot her a hard look. "You know as well as I that it's not good enough."

Ouch.

"That's not what she means," said Mama Vee, sitting down beside me. "Kiddo, I don't think you realize what you're up against."

Another creak. The eavesdropper was listening closely.

"After what you did last month, now more than ever, you need to be at your best," said Madame Moon.

"It's not that we think you're not up for the task," said Mama Vee. "If you were just going to be a babysitter like the others, we'd be thrilled."

Why can't I be just a babysitter? What more do they want from me?

Madame Moon gave Vee's compliment a begrudging wave. "You are an exceptional young woman, Kelly, and the order is lucky to have you." She leaned forward, her voice filled with grave concern. "But what you did on Halloween, defeating the Grand Guignol, one of the seven Boogeymen . . ."

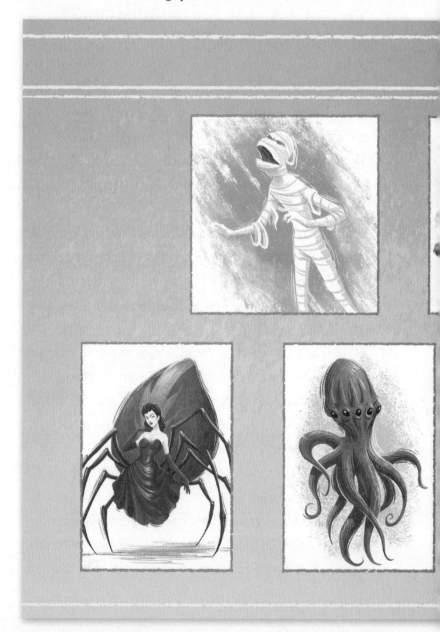

"Boogeypeople," I said under my breath.

"It changed everything. The other six are not going to take that lightly."

Cold tingles raced down my back.

The other six.

Vee clicked a button, and a large computer screen glowed with various images of the Boogeypeople.

I put that X there, I thought.

"I don't want to scare you," Vee said, "but you might have kicked off something far worse than any of us can imagine."

"You had better prepare yourself, Kelly," Madame Moon added, "because these monsters will seek their revenge."

Madame Moon slid a math textbook across the desk. I opened it to see that the pages had been cut out in order to hide a dagger with a wide blade. A jewel—a piece of jade—embedded in the handle swirled with a living cloud of strange, green light.

Vee peered out of the window overlooking the sweeping, wintry forest. I could see her reflection in the glass; the dire expression made my insides twist.

"It's time you understand, Kelly, that more monsters than ever are going to start coming out of the wood-work, looking to hurt you and everyone you love."

"Kelly? The answer?" demanded Mr. Flogger.

I snapped out of my daydream and rubbed my face. Algebra. Monday morning.

On my desk my math book was opened to chapter six: values of x and y. I squinted at the board where an equation read: $3x^3-4y^4 = -67$.

"Um," I said. "x is negative one and y is negative two?"

Mr. Flogger's tough glare softened. "That's right. Just try to stay awake."

It was the day after Heck Weekend, and I could barely keep my eyes open. Plus, being told you're being hunted by six of the deadliest monsters on the planet makes concentrating on school a teensy bit difficult.

Friday was our last day before Christmas break. And then it was one week of no school, cozy socks, hot chocolate with peppermint sticks and marshmallows, and the presents.

As I sleepwalked down the hall after class, I could feel the bubbly, electric anticipation fizzing among the kids and the teachers, who were united, if just for a few days out of the year, in their common desire to ride the Polar Express. But my muscles were so wrecked that I could barely lift my arm to open my locker. I stared blankly at my textbooks. I had a feeling this was going to be an interesting Christmas. And by interesting, I meant deadly.

"How was Heck Weekend?"

Victor stood beside me, brushing his shaggy black hair from his eyes.

Victor Cruz. My favorite Taylor Swift song. My supreme pizza with all the toppings. My knight in plaid and denim. My happy dance.

His smile filled me with sunshine.

"I'm alive. High five!" I said, holding up my hand.

He returned the five. "*¡Calidá!* I knew you'd survive."

His eyes sparkled with wonder whenever we spoke about the order. Victor wanted to know everything. Not the looking-after-little-kids part—which he said he knew about from growing up with a little brother and sister—just the part about the gory ghoulies.

"Wow. An official monster hunter," he said, shaking his head.

I exhaled heavily. I couldn't bring myself to tell him that I was not, in fact, voted babysitter of the year. But if you don't have anything nice to say about yourself, don't say anything at all, right?

"Oooooh, Victor, you're so hot!"

Victor's soccer buddies walked by, making kissing noises at us. Victor playfully kicked one of them in the butt, chasing them away.

"You have to let me babysit with you next time," he begged.

"Wouldn't you be embarrassed if the guys found out you helped me babysit?"

Everyone at our school treated the babysitters—Berna, Curtis, Cassie, and now me—like social misfits with a highly contagious freak disease. Not because we babysat, but because we were a little different from the rest of the herd. They had no idea how we actually spent our nights.

"I don't care what they think," Victor said.

I looked at him and sighed. He was so cool.

My heart fluttered, but then I remembered Mama Vee's reaction last week when I suggested Victor could come over while I babysat, to learn the ropes.

"The third law of babysitting, Kelly," Mama Vee had said with an amused smirk. "Check the guide."

Law Number One: protect your charge at all costs
Law Number Two: see Law Number One
Law Number Three: no crushes allowed while sitting

"Sorry, Victor," I said. "No crushes allow—" I said, catching the words before they could fall from my dumb mouth. "Did you do the chemistry homework? Because I did not."

"Huh?"

I laughed and shrugged. "What?"

He looked confused and then annoyed. He mumbled something in Spanish.

"What did you say?" I said.

"I didn't say anything," he said.

I looked at Victor. So sweet and wonderful. A terrible feeling grabbed me. Madame Moon's warning. If Victor hung out with me, he could get hurt. I wished I didn't have to worry about any of this stuff. I just wanted to eat pizza and binge-watch my new favorite TV show *A Time of Roses and Cattle* (from the producers of the hit South Korean soap opera *Tears of Flowers and Fish*) with him.

"Something wrong?" Victor asked.

I shook my head and tried to smile.

The stone in my throat got bigger, and I turned away as I wiped away a tear from my eye.

"Let's get this party started!"

Deanna, self-crowned princess and social media mogul, sashayed into the classroom. She was dressed like she was on a first-class ski trip to the Swiss Alps. I sniffed and wiped my faded orange sweater sleeve under my nose.

"*Hola*, Vicky," Deanna said, twinkling her fingers across the room at Victor. Victor rolled his eyes.

"Oh no! Kelly Ferguson, hast thou been crying, child?" Deanna shouted in mock sympathy. She waved a Kleenex at me, and I flushed red. "Vicky, what did you *do* to her?"

"I'm fine, Deanna," I growled. "And his name's Victor."

"Oooh, triggered!" said Deanna, dramatically dropping the Kleenex. "Some people are such snowflakes."

"Don't let her get to you," Victor whispered.

I boiled with anger until I imagined what would happen if Deanna talked to the Mighty Kang like that, and a wicked smile spread across my face.

"Yo, K-Ferg!" said Tammy, waving at me.

Tammy, my OG BFF from childhood, walked into class wearing not one but two fancy scarves, glittering jewelry, and a face full of makeup. I cocked my head in confusion. The Tammy I knew wore corduroys and

T-shirts that said "Bacon for Everyone!"

"Tamara!" ordered Deanna. "Sit next to me, fam."

Without even looking at me, Tammy sat in the seat next to Deanna.

I frowned. *"Fam"?* She's my fam! And hold on . . . *"Tamara"?* Tammy hated being called by her full name. She told me she thought Tamara sounded like a mean lady who yells at the butler and treats her prize-winning poodle better than her own children.

Tammy and I used to hang out every day, but ever since I became a babysitter, I had been spending more time with Berna, Liz, Mama Vee, Cassie, Curtis, and Victor. I didn't have the chance to tell Tammy the truth about babysitting, and if I'm being honest, I didn't want to. I needed her help on Halloween, and she bailed on me. Also, if she wanted to hang out with Deanna after Her Highness and her bedazzled tribe had trashed us for so long, then that's on her. The throbbing pain from warrior training was nothing compared to the scars I had from the mean insults Deanna and her clones had inflicted upon Tammy and me over the years.

At lunch I sat in the far corner of the cafeteria with Cassie, Berna, and Curtis. There were empty tables and chairs between us and the other students, forming a clear social divide. Cassie said she liked this quiet corner so we could speak freely about monsters, but I

46

knew it was because no one else wanted to sit near us.

"I can't believe you failed Heck Weekend," Curtis said.

Berna's elbow shot into Curtis's side. "Can't you see she feels bad enough? Don't rub it in that she failed. She probably feels like a failure, like nothing she does is good enough."

"Neither of you are helping right now."

"Then I guess we shouldn't give you this," said Curtis, sliding a small present wrapped in yellow paper with a bow on top across the table.

"We had them printed for you for finishing Heck Weekend," Berna said.

I tore it open. It was a stack of freshly printed business cards.

KELLY FERGUSON—BABYSITTER

KFergSitter13@gmail.com

My smile slowly fell. "Thanks, guys."

"You'll get there," said Berna, patting my hand. "Have a little faith. Right, guys?"

Cassie and Curtis agreed a little too eagerly. "Oh yeah. Totes! Totesh! Totes!"

"That's enough 'totes,' guys," I said.

I looked across the cafeteria to where Tammy was sitting with Deanna and the Princess Pack.

Tammy does look pretty with her fancy scarves and her shiny new earrings.

"Nothing wrong with trying a new look," said Berna. "But if she starts throwing shade at us like Deanna does, I am not gonna take it." Berna stabbed her fork into the mystery meat on her plate. "No way José. Berna does not abide."

That's another thing I liked about Berna. Even though she was nice, she took no baloney from anyone. Especially when it came to protecting her fellow babysitters.

"Deanna's pretty. Pretty people get away with being mean," said Curtis.

"That's no excuse. I'm beautiful and I'm nice, so explain that," Berna said with a smirk.

Cassie puffed out her cheeks. She looked so angry I thought she might pop. "You think Deanna'sh pretty?"

"Say it don't spray it, Cass," Curtis said with a chuckle, scooping mashed potatoes off his plate with his fingers.

"Ushe a fork, Curtish! Grossh!"

Curtis slurped the potatoes off his fingers. "What are you, my babysitter?"

"You wish!" Cassie flung a forkful of his own pota-toes in his face.

"What the hey, Cassie! I was making a point about the balance of the universe. What do you care if Dean-na's hot?"

Cassie threw the napkin dispenser at Curtis and stormed off.

"Ow! What crawled up her chimney?"

If Cassie liked Curtis, she had an odd way of show-ing it. Berna narrowed her eyes at Curtis. "Are you okay, Curtis? Like in the head?"

"I am so glad I'm not a girl," he mumbled.

"You should be so lucky," I said.

I held up my hand, and without even looking, Berna high-fived it. Boom.

Suddenly, all our phones chimed at the exact same time.

Liz had sent us a group text:

BS RI HQ. After school. Do it.

Berna scowled. "I can't. I have a track meet after school."

And I don't care if you have a track meet, Berna. Urgent.

"How does she do that?" said Berna.

Shrill echoes of death metal sped toward us. The school crossing guard craned his neck to see what the racket was. The babysitter mobile careened into view. A mismatched patchwork of metal siding covered up the bites and claw marks that had been ripped out of the van in the battle against the army of nightmares.

"I can't believe this thing still runs," said Curtis.

We waved good-bye to gawking teachers and piled into the back. Our monster buddy, a stout hobgoblin named Wugnot, high-fived us with his tail.

"Buckle up, babysitters," said Wugnot.

His claw stomped on the gas, and we shot off, spraying our middle school with a geyser of black exhaust.

"You really need to get a new ride, Wuggie," I said.

"It looks super shady getting picked up in this thing."

"You wanna walk? Be my guest," Wugnot said, veering us through traffic. "Besides, windows are tinted. They can't see my beautiful mug."

"I love this car," said Curtis, slapping the warped dashboard. "Can't wait till I'm old enough to drive so I can take it for a spin."

"Any time you want a lesson . . ."

"Wuggie, you are the last person who should be giving driving lessons," said Berna, almost vomiting in the back seat.

The hobgoblin let out a gruff chuckle.

We drove east, into the marshland. The van's giant tires splashed off road, bumping over rocks and ruins.

"Any idea what Liz needs to talk to us about?" I asked.

"Dunno. She won't say. She's in a real mood."

"When ish she not?" said Cassie.

"Cut her some slack," said Wugnot. "She's going through some things."

As we hurtled toward a wild thicket, Wugnot's tail pulled a knob on the dash marked "Voix Céleste" and a hornpipe on the van emitted a birdlike whistle. The thicket parted just in time for the van to fly through, thorns scraping the doors.

The van spun to a stop in front of HQ. A fluorescent green, off-road motorcycle was parked near a lion statue.

"Looks like Liz got a new ride from the *Penny-Saver*," said Curtis. "Suh-weet. Think maybe she'll let me take it off a few jumps?"

"No," we all said in unison.

Wugnot pulled open the big front door into a whirl-wind of shouting from Liz and Mama Vee.

"I'm going! You can't stop me!"

"Oh, yes I can!"

Liz and Mama Vee were arguing in the living room. Mounds of Liz's research materials were scattered around them. The terrifying 1793 portrait of Serena was leaning against the wall near the Christmas tree.

"I found where she's hiding, Vee!" screamed Liz. She slapped the map. "The cave of the Bell Witch. Tennessee. We need to go there right now."

"Wasn't her last marriage in New York?" I said.

"Divorce by death," Liz said quickly. "She was last seen down south."

"LeRue. Take a deep breath and calm down," ordered Vee.

Liz remained on her feet, panting. Mama Vee noticed us standing there and did a double take.

"What are you four doing here?" Vee asked.

We collectively shrugged.

"I called them here," said Liz.

Mama Vee shook her head in disbelief at Liz's blatant disregard for her rank. "One, this is in Tennessee.

I cannot authorize you traveling that far without super-vision."

"I don't need supervision—"

"Two, you have to babysit tonight."

"Someone else can fill in for me."

"Three, according to the head council, we cannot just barge into a Boogey's lair unprovoked."

"What do you call what we did on Halloween?"

"We had evidence. Read the bylaws."

"I've read the bylawsh," said Cassie, raising her hand like the teacher's pet.

"Not now, Cassie," said Mama Vee.

"This is an emergency," Liz said through her clenched teeth.

"We don't know that."

Liz leveled her eyes at Mama Vee. "Kevin's with her," she said.

"So let's gather intel first. We'll call the southern babysitters and have them take a look and report back. Then we'll strategize a plan and approach this the right way."

Liz's fingers curled into fists. "You don't think he's alive." Her voice was trembling.

I finally understood why Liz was so upset. She was holding on to a string of hope, and everyone else was telling her to let go.

"I never said that," Mama Vee replied gently. "This

53

is dangerous territory, Liz. We have to be smart."

Liz threw a stack of papers across the room. They fell like dead leaves.

"Smart? I found where she lives! What have you done?"

Mama Vee scowled. "My job. Which is to protect you, and if I say something is not right, it is not right. Now, look. You're too emotional and too obsessed. You lock yourself in the library all day and night. You stare at this creepy painting. You need to step back."

Liz grew eerily calm as she squinted at Mama Vee. She nodded to herself, as if she had made up her mind. She breezed past me and I reached out for her.

"Liz," I whispered.

Her eyes were fire. "You coming or what?"

The breath caught in my throat. On Halloween, I made her a promise and wanted to help her so badly, but something held me back. Maybe it was the fact that Tennessee was light-years away or maybe—*and I know this sounds super selfish*—it was because I didn't want to spend Christmas getting into deep, dark trouble.

"I'm not even a real sitter yet," I said.

She sneered sarcastically. "And you never will be." She grabbed her book bag and shoved open the front door.

"Liz LeRue, don't you dare!" screamed Mama Vee

as the sound of the dirt bike engine revved to life outside.

I ran through the front doorway and caught a faceful of gravel from Liz's spinning back tire. In a streak of green and black, she was gone. Mama Vee's angry shouts broke our stunned silence.

"Stop her, Wugnot," demanded Mama Vee.

Wugnot slid across the hood of the van and scrambled into the window. He sped off in a blast of death metal. Mama Vee turned on her heels and marched back inside.

"Liz wouldn't go all the way down there on her own, right?" said Berna, trying to assure Mama Vee. "I mean, all the way to Tennessee? On a motorbike. That's crazy. Even for Liz. She could get bugs in her teeth."

Mama Vee angrily cleaned up the mess Liz had made. The dog-eared books on spiders, the scattered obituaries, the maps. With each pile, she grew angrier, finally grabbing the leaning portrait. She was about to break it over her knee when she stopped and looked at its chilling crystal eyes. Serena seemed to be staring at Mama Vee with a knowing smile.

10

On the news the old farmer stood in a field of cows.

"I was sleeping last night when I heard the cowbells clanging," said the white-bearded farmer on TV. "I stumbled out of bed, grabbed my pants and my double-barrel, and I headed out here. That's when I seent it."

The old farmer pointed a shaking finger across a field of grazing cows.

"Must have been eight feet tall. Covered in brown and black hair." The farmer twisted his fingers around his forehead. "Two big ole horns. Didn't budge none. Just hid there, behind the trees, looking at me with them eyes. Thought 'twas a nightmare, till I found Bessie."

The news crew followed the farmer behind his

barn, where they found a mass of black flies buzzing around a sinewy pile of cow bones. The hide lay in the grass nearby like a discarded piece of black-and-white laundry.

"Now, you tell me, what kind of animal does that?"

"Oooooh," my dad said, his eyes glued to the TV in the living room. "Bigfoot's in Rhode Island!"

"It's probably some hoax," said my mom.

"Wouldn't that be cool, Kelly? Bigfoot in our own backyard!"

I forced a smile, but a dark fear crept inside me.

They're looking for you, Kelly.

On TV the disgusted reporter swatted flies with his microphone, sidestepping cow bones. I silently made a note: *Smithfield Farms. Seventy miles from here. Have to tell Mama Vee about this.*

"Turn on some real news," my mom said, adjusting an ornament on our thin Christmas tree.

"C'mon, Alexa. Kelly loves this stuff. Used to, anyway." My dad chuckled. "Remember when you were little, Kelly? We'd catch you staring out of your window, middle of the night. 'Daddy, I saw a monster.' So cute."

"That's me," I said, trying to sound cheery.

Our clock was draped with plastic garland and tinsel. It was twenty minutes to seven. "Shoot, I'm gonna be late."

I caught my mom and dad exchanging worried looks as I started for the dining room to clear the table.

"You're not babysitting tonight," said my mom, stretching up to straighten the crooked angel atop the evergreen.

"Veronica asked me to fill in for another sitter."

She followed me into the kitchen. "Kelly, your father and I are very proud of how hard you're working, but don't you think it's too much?"

"My grades are fine."

"I know. But look at you. The bags under your eyes. You look exhausted, honey."

"Haven't you heard?" I said. "Dark circles and pale skin are the latest fashion."

Steam rose from the hot water as I scrubbed the dishes. I felt my mother's stare fix on me.

"You're only young once, Kelly," my mom said. "Enjoy it. Before you know it, you'll have a family of your own. For now, just be a kid."

But I don't wanna just be a kid. Kids are small and puny, and they can't drive cars and they can't protect the ones they love from all the monsters in the world.

"I'm just trying to save up enough cash to go to Camp Miskatonic, Mom. So, if you think about it, all these babysitting jobs are so I can enjoy my childhood. Towel, please."

My mother finally relented, and later, she drove me to Middletown to my babysitting job. Ice streaked the windows, warping the passing houses' Christmas decorations into wavy rainbows. My phone buzzed. Babysitter group text:

CURTIS:
Just heard on police scanner. A blood truck got jacked last night!

CASSIE:
Waaaaaaat?

CURTIS:
Driver said small men wearing carnival masks did it.

BERNA:
Think it's Toadies?

KELLY:
Nope. Crushed 'em all. ;)

BERNA:
Trolls?

CASSIE:
Guide says Trolls don't do blood.

BERN:
Maybe 4 someone else?

"What's this about a van picking you and your friends up after school?" my mom said.

"Huh?" I said. "Oh. That's Veronica's car. I told you

about that. It's a clunker."

"You know, you can always talk to me or your father," my mom said in a concerned tone.

"One second, Mom."

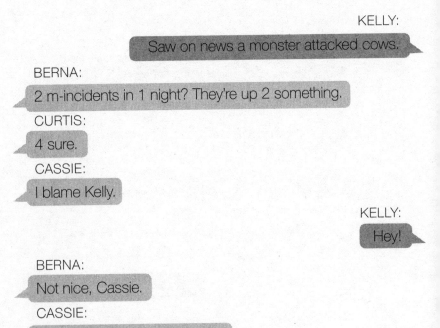

KELLY:

Saw on news a monster attacked cows.

BERNA:

2 m-incidents in 1 night? They're up 2 something.

CURTIS:

4 sure.

CASSIE:

I blame Kelly.

KELLY:

Hey!

BERNA:

Not nice, Cassie.

CASSIE:

Hey is for horses. Be on alert.

"Look. I get it," my mom said in her "I'm trying to be cool" voice. "I was thirteen once. It's a really weird time. Hormones. Your body is changing. Boys . . ."

I deleted the texts and let out a huge moan. "Puhlease, Mother. Not this."

"Not what?"

"The Talk. I don't need *The Talk*."

"Don't get huffy, Miss Thing. I'm just saying that last month you hated babysitting. Now it's all you do."

"Because you made me do it!" I snapped. "Remember when I just wanted to go to a stupid Halloween party, but you begged me to babysit your boss's kid!"

"Do not yell at me. I will turn this car around right now."

"I'm not yelling. I'm speaking with passion!"

It scared me how easily my anger flared up. It was good when hunting monsters but bad when trying to communicate with your parents.

"What is going on with you?" my mom said in a quiet voice.

"Nothing," I whispered.

But it wasn't nothing. Maybe Cassie was right. Maybe all of these monster incidents were somehow happening because of me. That's what I was really angry about, not my mom trying to talk with me.

We drove the rest of the way in silence. The tension was unbearable so I flicked on the radio.

"Bundle up, Rhode Island, it looks like winter's first nor'easter is on its way."

"Hopefully, tomorrow will be a snow day," I sighed.

"For both of us," Mom said.

We entered a street of sprawling apartment

61

complexes. A sign read "Welcome to Dakota Apartments." We passed rows and rows of the exact same buildings. Redbrick on the bottom, aluminum siding on top. The whole compound felt a little bleak and desolate.

"Who are you sitting for this time?" my mom said, squinting at the buildings.

I checked the info Mama Vee sent. "A woman named Dawn Harker and her son, Theodore."

"What do you know about her?"

"Just that she needs a babysitter, and she lives in building twenty-five, apartment two."

My mom made a disapproving grunt and parked in front of building twenty-five. Red bricks on the bottom, aluminum siding on top.

"Go and check it out, and if you get a weird vibe, give me a signal and I'll come get you."

I rolled my eyes, but I was secretly thankful for my mother's protective instincts. The sameness of the buildings reminded me more of a prison yard than a neighborhood. There was a single glowing Santa all alone in the front yard. Even jolly old Saint Nick looked miserable. I grabbed my backpack, pecked my mom on the cheek, and ran through the cold to a door with the number two stenciled on it.

After I jammed the buzzer a few times, the door flung open, and a woman wearing a burgundy Food

Time uniform with a name tag that read "Dawn" screamed in delight.

"Thank God you're here! Are you Kelly? You're Kelly, right? Gosh, you're young. Come in, come in, it's freezing out here. Is that your mom? Hi, Kelly's mom! Thanks for letting me borrow your daughter!"

Dawn gave a big wave. My mom smiled politely, waiting for me to give her the all clear. Dawn was frantic with upbeat, messy energy, and she was way younger than most of the parents I babysat for. She talked a million miles an hour, like she was getting ready for prom but didn't know what dress to wear. I liked her instantly.

I waved the all clear, and my mother shook her head and drove away. Dawn yanked me into the narrow staircase leading up to her apartment.

"So this is me," Dawn said, shoving a pile of laundry into the closet. Dirty dishes swarmed the sink. Colorful baby toys seemed to be her decoration of choice.

And I thought my room was a mess.

"Let me give you the grand tour," she said.

Dawn thrust out her arms and was able to reach into the kitchen, living room, and the hallway at the same time. A small, pink plastic Christmas tree was squeezed against the wall.

"Not exactly the Ritz, but it's home. Come meet the

little man." She crept into the dim bedroom and whispered, "I just fed him and put him to sleep."

A ceramic owl lamp cast a soft, gold glow upon a wall of butterfly wallpaper. A humidifier on the cabinet sent a steady plume of ethereal mist into the air. A music box played a twinkling lullaby. There was a quiet magic about the room. It felt like a sanctuary from the whole dreadful world outside.

There was a bassinet at the foot of a bed. Dawn's erratic pace slowed as she approached it. I leaned down with her to see a baby boy sleeping inside.

"That's Theo," she murmured.

Theo's little round head was covered in fine, soft hair. His button nose was perfect. He was smiling in his sleep. He totally had Dawn's dimples.

Sudden panic jolted through me.

That is a baby. You have never actually looked after a baby, even though it's in your job title. I thought I was looking after a kid—not a soft, helpless new-to-Earth creature.

Dawn kissed Theo's little forehead, and he gurgled. She motioned for me to sneak out of the bedroom.

"Whoa," I said.

Dawn smiled with pride.

"He's the greatest thing I've ever done. But he's also the hardest thing, too. It's like the stronger he gets, the more exhausted I feel. I'm worried he's some kind of vampire. Or he might just drive me totally crazy one day!"

She laughed and then suddenly burst into tears.

"Sorry, I was trying to make a joke, but I got a little real there for a second. You must be freaking out right now."

"Nope. I'm a professional," I said, trying to sound professional. Really, I didn't know whether to smile or run.

"I can tell that about you." She put her hands on her hips and crooked her jaw as she studied me. "Even though you're just a kid. I mean, heck, I'm only a few years older than you, right? You look smart and able. I get good vibes from you, Kelly."

"Thanks," I said.

"Anyhoooooo. I just fed him, so he'll probably be ready for a bottle in, like, two hours."

"Okay," I said, starting to feel overwhelmed.

"I pumped a ton earlier, so there should be plenty of milk for him in the fridge."

Pumped? What did she pump?

"Oh, and it might take a while for you to gas him. His burps are huge."

"Gas him"? How does one gas a child?

"Oh, and there's some baby oil. He likes a little on his butt. It's also good for if you have gum stuck in your hair, funny enough. Aaargh! I'm gonna miss my bus! My manager's gonna flip." She pulled on a heavy jacket and a woolly cap. "Call me if you need anything. But you'll be fine. I have total faith in you, Kelly."

That makes one of us!

"Oh, before I forget," I said, digging into my jacket.

I proudly presented Dawn with my very own business card.

"That's me!" I said.

"Cool beans," Dawn said.

She blew a kiss at the bedroom. "Good-bye, my little turtle. Mommy loves you."

I froze. "What did you just call him?"

"Sometimes when he yawns he looks just like a turtle. It's freaking adorable. You'll see."

Dawn dashed from the apartment. I was immobile.

The Mighty Kang's voice rang through my mind. *Protect the turtle hatchling. The turtle will bring peace to the world of sssssun and air.*

11

A shrill, piercing scream rang from the bedroom. Theo the angel had become Theo the devil in two seconds flat. When I ran to his room, I saw that his face was tomato red as his cry ripped through me.

"Shhh, don't cry, Baby Theo, don't cry," I said.

"RRRREEEAAAAAAAH! AAAAH! EEEEUU! RAAARAAAA!" the baby screamed in my face.

When my attempt at baby talk failed, I scooped him up and held him in my arms. I went a little deaf with his mouth beside my ear.

Whatever you do, do not drop him.

I popped Theo's pacifier into his mouth, and the

floodgates closed. He burbled happily, making gentle suckling noises.

Phew.

My ear was still ringing. I gently set him down in his bassinet, but the moment I left the room, he exploded into a shrieking fit. I scooped him up again, and I felt his little heart beating. All he really wanted was to be held.

I turned on the television in the hopes of distracting him (and in the hopes I could watch something other than the screaming baby channel). I saw three seconds of *Frosty the Snowman* before he nixed it. Balancing Theo in my arms, I reached for my phone and called Liz.

"What do you want, Ferguson?" I could hear the grinding of her dirt bike engine in the background.

"Liz?! Where are you?"

"Somewhere outside Philadelphia!" Liz shouted.

Wind crashed over the phone. I imagined Liz speeding on her bike down Route 95.

"I hope you have ice in your hair and bugs in your teeth. Because of you, I'm babysitting a freaking newborn!"

"Theo's supercute, isn't he?"

"He's the most beautiful thing I've ever seen but that's beside the point!"

Theo fidgeted and accidentally head butted my chest. This kid didn't have the best neck control.

"Liz. I can't do this. I need your help."

"The only baby there is you, Ferguson. Just don't drop him and check the guide."

Check the guide. Her answer for everything.

"Liz," I pleaded. "Please come back. I'm worried about you."

"Then you shouldn't have bailed on me."

My heart sank with guilt. "I can't just drive across the country. I'm thirteen."

"Have fun with the kid. He's full of surprises."

"What does that mean?"

The line went dead. Theo squirmed in my arms. Another crying jag was coming on. I frantically opened my backpack and took out my copy of the *Babysitter's Guide to Monster Hunting*.

BABIES (HUMAN)

The human baby requires a babysitter's utmost care and full attention. Do not take your eyes off her/him for a second. This task is not to be taken lightly and should be performed by an experienced professional.

BASIC BABY NEEDS:

- A warm bottle of formula or breast milk
- Burping after bottle
- A clean diaper and bottom
- Must be given attention, love, and affection at all times.
- Must be kept warm at all times. Blanket or swaddle

SPECIAL PRECAUTIONS:

- Some monsters are attracted to the smell of a dirty diaper, so dispose of properly and change often.
- Never leave a baby unattended.
  Word of advice: don't panic. Babies are stressful. Stay as calm as you can for as long as you can.
- As they are brand-new to this Earth, their brains and hearts are completely open to all things unseen. Some even have a magical, rare ability to detect even the slightest supernatural presence.

   NOTE: If baby is crying endlessly, see section marked the Witching Hour.

I flipped the guide to *W*.

THE WITCHING HOUR

A time of night when a baby cries and nothing—no bottle, no swaddle, no burp, no gripe water, no teething ring—can stop him/her. This dreaded time is known as the Witching Hour.

While some believe this time of fussiness to be the result of a gassy belly or a poopy diaper, experts believe the Witching Hour is the time when a newborn is most attuned with the unseen realms of ghosts, ghouls, and creatures of the night.

So if the baby you are looking after begins wailing in the dead of night after all his/her needs have been met, check under the bed, make sure the windows and doors are locked, and protect that little one because a monster looking for its next meal is sure to be lurking nearby.

Theo's breathing had grown quiet and peaceful. He kept squeaking and smacking his lips in his sleep. The guide failed to mention that babies sounded like squirming piglets.

He stretched and yawned with a gummy smile. My eyes widened. Little Theo *did* look just like a turtle.

"I might not know what I'm doing, Turtle, but I'll do my best to protect you. Yes I will, Bubsa! Yes, I will!"

His lips curled up into a huge smile.

"Eeeoooaaah!" squealed Baby Theo. "Oooooaaaa."

"Yes, that's right. Ooooooaaaa, Bubsa! Aren't you a smart little bubby wub wubs. And we're going to have funny fun-fun times, yes we are, yes we are." Don't judge me. It's impossible not to talk like this when you're in the vicinity of a cute baby. "Who's a little turtle wurtle? That's right! You are, Bubsa booty! And who has the cutest little birthmark?"

I saw a birthmark on the side of his chubby little drumstick leg. It was larger than most birthmarks, with a circle and a small nub sticking out from under it.

"It looks like . . ."

I squinted. It was in the shape of a turtle shell.

12

A rumbling erupted in Theo's diaper. My hand went warm.

It was time for me to learn how to change a diaper while changing a diaper. I'll spare the description of the mustard-colored horror that awaited me. Just know that I managed to do it.

Chirp-chirp. Victor was FaceTiming me. I swatted my hair back and answered it.

Victor was in his bedroom, adjusting a lamp away from his face. His room was filled with soccer star posters, and an empty aquarium sat behind him.

"Hiya," Victor said, brushing his hair out of his eyes.

"Hey, you!"

"What are you up to?"

"Changing diapers. Living the dream."

I aimed the phone over Theo so Victor could see him.

"Angelito," Victor gasped. "That's a beautiful little dude."

I smiled at his adoration. "Hope our kids are that cute," I said.

"What?"

"Nothing! How are you doing?" I angled the phone to show my good side. I should win an Oscar for best cinematography for the work I put into FaceTiming with Victor.

He showed me his half-finished chemistry homework. "Chemistry. It's impossible."

"I loathe chemistry," I said.

"Wanna help me?"

"I'm babysitting."

He smirked mischievously and his eyebrows jumped. "I could come over."

A happy dolphin did a backflip in my stomach. But then I remembered Babysitting Law Number Three: *thou shalt have no crushes over while on duty.*

"You do know I grew up taking care of my little brother and sister, right? I was ten and I changed all sorts of diapers," Victor said. "I'm like the *bebé* whisperer."

My eyes lingered on his eyes. Could this guy be any

more adorable? I propped the phone up so we could still FaceTime while I held Theo. I wanted to show Victor my baby skills, but Theo thrashed, flailing his arms and legs.

"Try singing," Victor said.

I desperately bounced Theo up and down while singing a nonsense tune. Victor sang a little something, too. He had such a rich voice.

Still, Theo wailed.

Something's wrong.

"Try a toy?" Victor said.

I hope that's what's wrong.

I grabbed a plastic teething ring. Theo found an even higher octave to cry in.

"I'm worried his head is going to pop off," I said.

"Sometimes babies just cry for no reason," Victor said.

I looked around the room.

Or they cry because a monster is nearby. . . .

"Hey, what is that?" he said, pointing.

My hand shot to my nose. Did I have a booger this whole time? In the FaceTime screen, I saw something waving behind me. I squinted into the small selfie square. I could see me, Theo, the room behind me, and the window. Something outside was looking in.

I spun around. Six bloodshot eyeballs lingered in the window, staring directly at me, eyestalks waving just above the sill like slimy periscopes. I gasped and clung to the baby.

"What is that?" Victor said.

Be cool, Kelly. You've done this before.

I wheeled Theo's bassinet into the living room. First things first: get Theo out of harm's way. His crying subsided for a moment. I shut the bedroom door and stood alone with the thing outside the window.

The giant eyeballs left smudge marks as they bumped against the glass.

My mind raced. *I've never seen anything like that thing. We're two floors up. Means it can climb walls. Breathe, Kelly. Keep cool. At least it's a monster and not a bug.*

"Go away!" I yelled, flailing my arms.

"I'm not hanging up with you!" I heard Victor's voice.

"Not you, it!" I said.

"Let me see!" he begged.

Ugh, Victor! I grabbed my phone and stood it up so Victor could see the lurking creep.

"Deees-gusting!" said Victor, excited.

I took a big step toward the window to show it that I wasn't afraid.

"By the Order of the Rhode Island Babysitters, I command you to leave the premises!" My voice quivered.

The gray, sluglike globes remained locked on me

76

with an unsettling gaze. I flicked open my camera app and snapped a few pics. Its spongy, oversized meatball body was clinging to the second-floor wall by a slime-dripping sucker.

"What is it?" Victor whispered.

Look it up later. Right now just get rid of it.

I tossed my phone and unzipped my book bag. My copy of S. E. Hinton's *The Outsiders* spilled out.

So much for finishing that book report.

My hands fluttered over my babysitter arsenal that's been disguised to look like kid's stuff (in case anyone looked inside). A bag of exploding jelly beans? I couldn't see a mouth to throw them into. A jump rope that expanded into a net? I had zero desire to catch this creep. A rubber ducky with an earsplitting squeaker? Don't want to wake the baby. A silver dagger hidden in my math textbook? Too messy.

Finally, I found a Barbie doll tucked into the side pocket. She had high-powered electrodes hidden in her head. One squeeze, and a bolt of electricity would shoot ten thousand volts from Barbie's eyes. Perfect.

"Get lost or get fried, Six-Eyes!"

I shook the doll's blond head at the meatball. Not my most threatening pose.

With my body pressed against the wall, I reached out to open the window. Six glistening eyestalks slithered toward me. I aimed, yanked back on Barbie's hair, and a lightning bolt blasted from her eyes. The monster squealed. Its electrified tentacles whipped like fire hoses. It fell two floors down and landed with a wet *smack.*

I leaned out, expecting to see a splattered goo puddle, but the creature was bouncing, very much alive. Its peepers retracted into its round, squishy body. Like a living bowling ball, it rolled across the lawn, noisily knocking over trash cans before wobbling into the night.

I slammed the window, locked it, and pulled down the blinds. Smoke rose from Lightning Barbie's melted face. I shook my head in disbelief. My hands were shaking.

What was that thing and why was it here?

Baby Theo was still sleeping safe and sound in the living room. I picked him up and held him. I think I needed the hug more than he did.

"Kelly? You okay?" Victor kept asking on FaceTime.

"I'm cool," I said quietly.

"I wish I was there." The excitement was gone from his voice.

I wanted to stay on the phone with him, but I had work to do. I said good-bye, put little Theo in a baby swing, and grabbed my red spiral-bound *Babysitter's Guide to Monster Hunting.*

NAME: Six-Eyed Sleeknatch
(foR Five-Eyed Fungi, see page 23)

ABILITIES: wall cRawling, night vision, extRaoRdinaRy heaRing, telepathic communication with otheR monsteRs

LIVES: The jungles of Cambodia, tRopical climates

STRENGTHS: TheiR squishy skin makes them Resilient to most weapons. Because of its RemaRkable eyes and eaRs, the Sleeknatch is most commonly employed by otheR monsteRs to obseRve intended victims.

WEAKNESSES: Common table salt seems to be the only thing that does any Real damage. It dehydRates them beyond RepaiR.

I swallowed hard. According to the guide, Sleeknatches live in tropical jungles. That meant it was far from home. Someone brought it here to look for something. Most likely me or Theo.

How long did I have before more monsters would show up looking for revenge?

13

Dawn's apartment seemed like it was getting smaller. The heater was turned up so high I felt like I was sitting in front of a hair dryer.

I called Berna and told her everything.

"Maybe I'm just being paranoid," I said.

"I'm on my way," Berna said.

"It's late, Berna. You don't have to come."

"Sitters look out for one another, Kelly. Besides, I live close by. Give me ten."

Luckily, there was nothing in the rule book about another babysitter coming over in an emergency.

Baby Theo started to cry again. Loud, hard, angry. The same red-faced fury as when the Sleeknatch showed up. I gulped. Either his crying jag before was a total coincidence, or . . .

My heart pounded as I rocked him in my arms and checked the windows. The lonely glow of fluorescent lights hovered in the distance. Someone wearing a long fur coat crossed the frosty lawn and ducked quickly behind the next building over. I stopped breathing.

I watched the edge of the nearby building. Theo screamed in my arms. I shushed him and patted him on the back. I could make out the silhouette of two branches swaying around the corner of the distant apartment building. Squinting, my eyes strained in the dark. No, they were not branches. They were two scraggly horns—one was broken at the tip—twisting from the head of a creature covered in fur. Icy breath steamed from its snout as its pure silver eyes locked on me.

The buzzer rang. Berna! She was out front, and she had no idea this hulking beast was in the back! Cradling Theo, I jumped to the intercom and jabbed the unlock button. I heard the lock click downstairs as I peered out the window. The giant hairy monster was gone.

"Where'd it go?" I whispered.

Slow, heavy footsteps clomped up the stairs. A sickly dread ran down my spine. What if that wasn't Berna at the front door? What if I had just buzzed up a monster?

Thump, thump. The steps stopped.

I stared at the locked door, holding Theo close as I reached into my book bag. The baby gurgled gently now, grabbed a fistful of my hair, and put it in his mouth.

"You're not crying, so does that mean it's okay?" I asked the baby.

Theo's big blue eyes stared up at the ceiling, as if it were the most interesting thing in the entire world.

"Kelly? You in there?" I heard Berna call from behind the door.

"Is that really Berna?" I yelled.

"Of course it's me! Who else would it be?"

"What's your favorite Friendly Unicorn?"

"Princess Stardazzle. Because of her loyalty and rainbow healing powers."

I unlocked the door and hugged Berna with my free arm.

"What's going on, Kelly?"

I pulled Berna to the window and pointed to the spot where the horned creature was lurking.

"A monster was right there. Just now!"

Berna's mouth hung open so wide her gum almost fell out. "I rode my bike right by there. I could've been monster meat!"

"I think it's gone," I said.

"How do you know?"

I held Theo up. "He stopped crying."

"We need to go out there and collect samples."

"Outside? That's like the beginning of every horror film. We need to stay inside where it's cozy and warm."

Berna cocked her head to the side and raised her eyebrows. "Don't act scared with me. I didn't come here to eat chips and talk boys and watch some awful TV show with subtitles. You and I both know we need to go out there, collect data, gather evidence, and see what we're up against. Now bundle up that baby and let's hit the scene."

I turned Theo into a baby burrito of blankets and followed Berna down the stairs.

"Normally, I wouldn't be this freaked out," I whispered, "but I'm worried about the baby."

"Whatever you say." Berna smirked.

Berna peered out across the grounds and gave me the all clear. Our breaths turned to icy mist as we crossed the sprawling lawn. Frosty grass crackled under our sneakers. Theo's little nose was red, but he was warm in my arms. I scanned the night, praying nothing would jump out at us.

"See that? Right there!" Berna opened her backpack and removed a pair of tweezers and a glass vial. She plucked a clump of hair from one of the bricks and dropped it into the jar, screwing the lid on tight.

"See any scat?" Berna asked.

"Scat?"

"Y'know, droppings. Helps identify the thing."

Berna handed me her guide. It was neatly organized with page dividers and little color-coded tabs. She opened it to a laminated diagram of monster poop. "You don't have one of these?"

"Nope. But now I know what to ask for Christmas," I said.

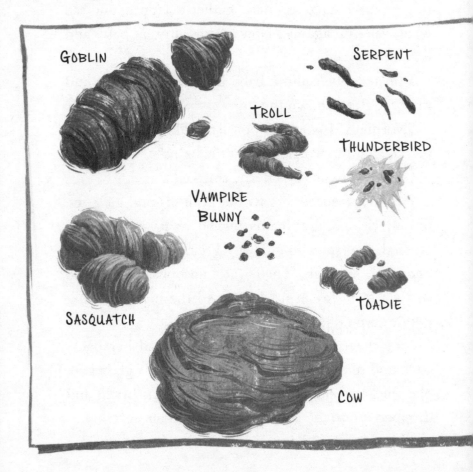

"Aha! Look, there's Squatch poo," said Berna.

Berna tucked her scat chart and her evidence kit into her backpack. As we collected a sample from the Sleeknatch's slime trail, something flashed in the lone, dead tree where I first saw the wanna-be bigfoot. I slowly walked toward it, listening for any signal from Theo. A piece of metal in the middle of the tree glinted in the moonlight. Tucked inside the tree's hollow knothole was a toy soldier.

I plucked the pewter figurine and held it up to the light. It looked like a World War Two soldier firing a bazooka. A long, brown-and-black hair was stuck to the soldier's foot. Scratches and scuffs marred the surface. Under the base were lines that looked like maybe they could be writing, but they were too worn and faded for me to tell.

Was it a gift? A threat? A game?

As Berna tweezed the scraggly hair into a glass evidence vial, my whole body shivered. Maybe it was the chill December night, or maybe it was the feeling that the hairy, horned monster had left it there for me to find, as if sending me a message: *I found you.*

The *Babysitter's Guide to Monster Hunting* had no matches for the horned beast. Bigfoot, yes. Sasquatch, all day. But this specific creature, *nada*.

"Is that your book report, Kelly?"

I slapped the guide shut. My English teacher, Mr. Gibbs—or as he kept trying to nickname himself, Captain Red Beard—was staring at me with raised eyebrows.

English class. Tuesday morning.

Get it together, Kelly!

I jammed the guide into my backpack and fished out my half-finished book report on S. E. Hinton's *The Outsiders*. Beads of sweat rose from my forehead.

I had every intention of finishing my book report

last night, Mr. Gibbs, but I was distracted by monsters stalking me, was what I wanted to say.

What I actually said was, "I'll be done with it tomorrow."

Mr. Gibbs clicked his tongue. "See me after class."

I sank into my seat. I had never missed a homework assignment in my life. I heard Deanna whisper something to Tammy, and Tammy giggled. I could feel Victor watching me with sympathetic eyes. His empathetic look made me feel even more like a failure.

After class, Mr. Gibbs sat at his desk and snacked on baby carrots.

"What's up with you, Kelly?" he said between noisy chews. "You're one of my brightest students, but lately, you've been kinda spacey."

"I read the book; I just need to finish the report. Can I make it up?" I begged. "Please, Captain Red Beard?"

"No. But points for using my nickname. Have a carrot."

"I can explain. Okay. I can't really explain. But—"

"I'm going to have to give you an F."

I gasped. The earth went wobbly under my feet. "I've never gotten an F in my life!"

"Welcome to the club," said Mr. Gibbs. "Word of advice, it's not a very good club to be in."

No kidding.

Dazed, I walked into the hall.

You're not good enough, Kelly. You're going to fail, Kelly. You're not qualified to do this, Kelly. Just give up.

Victor was waiting for me outside.

"What's with the carrot?"

I tossed the carrot into the trash. "I got an F."

"Congratulations!"

I shook my head and walked to the cafeteria. I wasn't in the mood to ironically celebrate being a loser. Victor waited with me in line for Taco Tuesday.

"You don't have to sit with me," I said, not wanting him to see me like this. "You can sit with your friends."

"Aren't you my friend?" he said.

And now I've been friend-zoned! Wow. I can't do anything right.

I guess I had a pretty sad puppy-dog expression on my face because he cleared his throat and changed the subject to ice-skating as we sat at a corner table.

"One winter, it got so cold that Milton's Pond froze," I said, trying to inject some fun into our awkward chit-chat. "Tammy and I skated on it. It was a total *Charlie Brown Christmas* moment."

"Milton's Pond? I live near there. If it freezes again, maybe we can go, over break. Like a . . ."

Like a date? Is he about to say like a date? SAY IT! SAY IT!

"Kelly! Kelly!"

88

Cassie stomped up to our table. "Schcoot over, I have to talk you. Schcoot!"

I growled as she elbowed her way into the seat next to me.

Who am I kidding? Victor wasn't going to ask me on a date. We're just friends.

"Misshush Merkowitzh ish letting ush ushe the microshcope in the schience room," Cassie whispered. "We're inveshtigating the hairsh you found."

Because Berna was her star pupil and always offered to clean the board and organize text books, Mrs. Merkowitz would let her eat lunch unsupervised in her room. Mrs. M had no idea that her science room had become a secret satellite office for the babysitters.

"Can Victor come?"

Cassie glared at Victor. He made a "pretty please" gesture.

"He knows, Cass," I whispered. "He was there on Halloween, and he saw the Sleeknatch last night."

Cassie fixed her crazy eyes on his. "Do you shwear yourshelf to shecreshy before the order, punishable by death?"

"With all my heart," Victor said, holding up his hand.

"Fine. But no talking."

The lingering smell of pickled frog guts lingered in Mrs. Merkowitz's science room. There was even an emergency shower in the back of the room, *just* in case a kid caught fire in an experiment gone wrong. Science class was a constant reminder that nature was always trying to kill you.

We found Berna and Curtis in the back room, where Mrs. M kept all the expensive gear. We closed the door, and the sweet scent of Wild Berry Bubble Rush filled the air as Berna cracked her gum while peering into a high-powered microscope.

"I looked up the horned monster in the guide," I said. "Couldn't find a match."

"Me neither," said Curtis.

"This might help us identify him. Take a look," Berna said.

I squinted into the scope and saw a single strand of the beast's brown hair magnified a thousand times. Among its ridges and grooves were chunks of stuff clinging to the sides. Berna cracked her gum quickly, which meant her  mind was in overdrive. Victor eagerly sat in the corner.

"It has the usual stuff attached to it. Mud and fauna. Except . . . ," Berna trailed off. Either she was holding something back or her mind was racing into sixth gear.

She switched out the hair slide for one with a tiny speck on it. Under the scope, it looked like a massive gray rock.

"There was one element that I couldn't quite place."

"Some kind of stone?" I asked.

"If you look close, you'll see it's not just ordinary sediment or rock. It's limestone with quartz and pyrite. See the white pressure lines there? It also has graphite and a hint of iron oxide. This is marble."

I glanced up from the microscope. "How the heck do you know that?"

"Everyone knows that's what marble's made of," she said.

"No one knows what marble's made of, Berna," I said.

Berna shrugged and pointed at the slide. "What's really interesting is that this particular type of marble isn't from the United States. It's from Italy."

We all stared at Berna in disbelief. She blew a huge, blue bubble.

"Okay, *seriously*. How do you know that?"

"Because she's Berna!" Curtis said.

"Guys, it's simple. This type of quartz is only found in the mines of Tuscany. And this type of marble hasn't been sold for a hundred years," Berna said.

"Like what they build *palacios*—mansions—with?" Victor exclaimed.

Berna tapped her finger to her temple and then pointed at Victor. "Beauty and brains."

"I told you not to talk," Cassie scowled at Victor.

"Ignore her," Curtis said. "It's good to have another dude here. Jerky?"

Curtis held out a piece of dried red jerky.

"Thanks," said Victor, taking a bite.

"It's squirrel jerky," Curtis said. "My dad's teaching me how to make it. Once you get past the fuzzy parts, it's pretty good."

Victor gagged. We all laughed.

"I should've warned you. Never eat Curtis's lunch," I said.

Victor forced himself to swallow. He smacked his lips, and his eyes brightened. *"Delicioso."*

Curtis cackled and slapped Victor on the back. "Good man! Have another, bro!"

Cassie giggled. Berna nudged me: *This guy's okay.* Victor took another bite of rodent bark and winked at me. My cheeks went warm. I looked back to the microscope and tried to focus.

"We can't know for sure if the monster is hiding at a mansion," I said. "It might have just been walking by and grazed the side or something."

Berna popped her gum. "The placement of the marble fragment on the hair was closer to the root. Not the end. Which means our furry friend is spending enough time at this *palacio* to get those fragments deep within its fur."

"So you think a yeti is living in a mansion?" said Victor.

"First off, yeti are snowbound creatures," said Curtis in a superserious tone. "And Squatches are primarily in the Pacific Northwest. It could be a Lurker, but they travel in packs."

"Squatch?" Victor said.

"Short for Shashquatch. Doy!" Cassie said.

Victor nodded. I could see he was a little freaked out.

"What about the Sleeknatch slime?" I said. "Anything on it?"

Berna handed me the vial of the spying meatball monster's yellowy slime we had collected.

"I'll let you do the honors."

I dripped a spot on a glass slide and peered at it under the microscope. All sorts of bits floated in the murky pool of goo. Among them were flecks of the same marble rock Berna had found on the beast's hair.

"I think they're roommates," I said.

Berna looked into the microscope.

"Ladies and germs, we have a match," Berna said.

The bell rang. We cleaned up our slime and hair samples and walked out of the back room.

Cassie took out her phone. "I'll run a shearch on

all the manshionsh in the area built with Tuhshcan marb– AAAWK!"

Cassie's feet shot out from under her, and she hit the linoleum. Hard.

"Have a nice trip?" Curtis giggled. "See you next fall!"

"It'sh not funny, Curtish!" shrieked Cassie, clutching her elbow in pain. Victor quickly scooped up Cassie. Curtis offered his hand to help her, but then he slipped and smashed into the floor.

I saw what they had slipped on. A pool of murky yellow slime wound across the floor. With growing panic, I followed the slick goo trail under the tables to the back of the classroom, where it vanished down the drainpipe under the emergency shower.

The Sleeknatch had been here, watching our every move.

15

I ran down the hall, pulling the straps on my book bag tight. Berna, Cassie, Curtis, and Victor ran to keep up with me.

"No running in the halls!" yelled Vice Principal Flowers. "Ready, set, slow!"

We stopped running and briskly walked together.

"You guys," I said. "That thing's here for me. I'm not going to sit back and wait for it to attack me. I'm going to find and stop it before . . ."

The words caught in my throat. My attempt at sounding brave screeched to a halt.

"Before it hurts anyone," I said quietly.

"Should we ditch school?" Curtis said hopefully.

"No way!" I said. "I already got an F on an English

assignment today. And that'll bring my grade down to a B minus. If I skip a class, I fail that class, and I need to get all As if I want to get a scholarship to a good college."

"College?" said Victor. "We're in middle school."

"I like to plan ahead," I said.

"Girl's got priorities," Berna said.

Cassie gasped, her lower lip dripping saliva as she stared at her phone. "You guysh! I found five manshionsh that were built with the shame shtone we found. Closhest one ish at Fifty-Five Bellevue Court."

"We'll run the GSC play," Berna said, flipping through her guide.

"GSC?" I asked.

"Girl Scout cookies. Basically, we pretend to be Girl Scouts selling cookies," Berna said. "That way no one suspects us of snooping around while Curtis flies his drone and takes pictures."

"Got the uniformsh and everything," Cassie added proudly.

"I hate the GSC play." Curtis sighed.

"I bet you look great in a brown skirt, Curtis," I said.

Berna snickered and fist-bumped me.

"Hardy har. No. I always have to play the supportive brother, and you guys make me carry all the cookies."

"Becaush you're sho shtrong," Cassie said, batting her eyelashes at Curtis.

Curtis made a goofy laugh and playfully shoved Cassie. Berna pretended to puke.

"So can I come?" Victor asked.

"Sorry, bro," said Curtis. "Girl Scouts only."

I took Victor aside. "It's too dangerous. I don't want you getting hurt."

"I don't get hurt. I do the hurt," he joked, smacking his fist in his palm.

I shook my head. He was not coming, no matter how charming he was.

Victor clenched his jaw. "When you look at me, what do you see?"

"Dimples?"

Victor growled and walked off.

"Was that a trick question?" I called after him, but he was gone.

Berna, Cassie, and Curtis were all watching my crash and burn. I threw up my hands. "I try to protect him, he hates me. I don't protect him, he might get eaten by a monster. I can't win."

"Love and monsters, man," Curtis said, shaking his head. "They just don't mix."

Cassie looked shocked. "What'sh that shupposhed to mean?" She punched Curtis in the arm. Hard. And then she stormed off to class.

"Ow!" Curtis cried. "What did I say?"

"If you don't know, we can't help you," Berna said.

We walked to class, leaving an utterly confused Curtis rubbing his arm.

After school, thick gray clouds hung low in the sky. The clang of the rope rang against the frozen flagpole. I was inside, by the doors facing the parking lot, keeping an eye out for the Sleeknatch, when Cassie quickly approached me.

"Can I ashk you shomething, Kelly?" Cassie said.

Her voice sounded humble and quiet. Not like its usual bossy tone.

"It'sh about boysh. One boy. I won't shay who. You don't know him," she said.

I nodded, pretending like I had no idea she was talking about Curtis.

"I like him, but he doeshn't know it. Or if he doesh know it, he doeshn't care. What should I do?"

I felt honored Cassie would ask me. Then again, I had no clue what to tell her.

"I think Curtis likes you; he just doesn't know how to show it."

Cassie's cheeks flushed red. Her eyes darted around. "How did you know it wash him?"

"Lucky guess."

"How do you know he likesh me?" she whispered with a growing smile.

"He laughs at your jokes. He hangs out with you all the time."

98

"He jusht needsh a little push ish what you're shaying?"

"That's not what I'm saying. Just take your time. Be friends—"

"Quiet! Here he comesh!"

Cassie and I straightened up as Curtis and Berna walked over.

"What were you guys talking about?" said Berna, looking between us suspiciously.

"Shoesh," said Cassie.

"Monsters," I said.

Curtis snorted. Cassie shot me a look, as if to say, *Not a word of this to anyone!*

The shrill sounds of heavy metal shrieked outside. Wugnot and the babysitter mobile had arrived. We darted across the icy parking lot and hopped into the back of the chugging van. It was warm in there. Thick with the smell of peppermint.

"Fifty-Five Bellevue Court, please, Wugnot," I asked our hobgoblin driver.

The passenger seat swiveled around to reveal Mama Vee, hair tied up in a big red scarf, eyes locked on me.

"Where do you think you're going?" she said.

"On a hunt?" I replied.

"You look awful, kiddo. And I don't mean that in a mean, superficial way. I mean that in an 'I am genuinely concerned about your well-being' way."

Wugnot snorted. Vee was right. I was so jacked up on adrenaline that I had forgotten how soggy and heavy my body felt. She poured a steaming cup of tea from her thermos and handed it to me.

"You go into the field now, and you could make some serious errors. You're already in hot water with your folks. So, the only place you're going is home for the three Ss: snack, study, sleep."

"Why are you acting like I'm five years old and you're still my babysitter?" I said.

"Because you're not even a real sitter yet, Kelly. Or did you forget that?"

Ouch.

"Thanks for reminding me," I said, setting down the teacup. "FaceTime if you find anything," I said to Berna before storming out of the van.

Sitting in the yellow school bus of shame, I dialed Liz's number and left her a long, rambling message. I hung up and stared out of the window. Houses and streets blurred together in a gray streak with the occasional green and red and gold of Christmas decorations. I closed my eyes and leaned forward, letting the cold glass soothe my hot forehead.

"What's shaking, K-Ferg?"

Tammy was staring at me from the next seat over. I pulled my scarf tightly around my neck. "Hey, *Tamara.*"

Tammy groaned as if she was soooooo embarrassed and yet it was all soooo hilarious.

"You used to hate that name," I said.

Tammy straightened up, defensive. "Still my name."

Her gold shimmer eye shadow, dark brown eyeliner, and bright red lipstick made her look like she was sixteen. And she was wearing glitter, so help me, *glitter*. She looked awesome.

"Your mom lets you wear makeup now?"

Tammy's eyes widened. "No! Thanks for reminding me. Yikes, Phyllis would blow a rod if she saw me wearing this. Deanna did it after first period."

She wiped a Kleenex across her lips and eyes, smearing the vibrant colors into thick smudges. Seeing Tammy used to make me feel silly and light, as if we were back in first grade. Now it just made me sad.

"Here," I said, offering her a pack of moist baby wipes I kept in my book bag.

"Thanks," she said, checking her face in her phone. "Guess being a babysitter has its perks after all, huh?"

I cut right to it. "Are you embarrassed that I hang out with the babysitters, Tammy?"

Tammy avoided my gaze. "I didn't say that. It's just . . . they're a little off."

"Actually, they're on. They're awesome in every way."

"What is going on with you? No offense, but you look rough. Are you okay?"

Even though we weren't the best of besties anymore, I wanted to tell her everything, but I didn't want her getting hurt.

"I'm the best I've ever been," I said, shoving my shoulders back. "Just wondering why you're hanging out with a girl who has bullied and tormented us for the past five years of our lives. That's all."

"We got partnered up in science class, and I made her laugh, I guess. Deanna's not that bad," Tammy said.

"Tammy, in fourth grade, Deanna tweeted a rumor that you had a supercontagious skin condition that made your skin peel off like a snake. For a year nobody would sit next to you except me. Or remember that time she tripped me in the hall and I chipped my front tooth?"

Tammy narrowed her eyes. "Maybe I'm an undercover agent plotting our revenge against her."

"Or maybe you just decided you like hanging out with the beautiful, popular kids because you think they'll make you beautiful and popular," I snapped.

Tammy blinked quickly. I knew that look too well. Tears usually followed it.

"That came out harsher than I wanted," I added, cringing. "I meant to say just be you."

She snorted and shook her head. "Look," Tammy said. "Maybe this *is* me and that other Tammy was just a stepping-stone on my evolution to my best self."

I rolled my eyes. She was even talking like Deanna.

For the rest of the bus ride, she cycled through Instagram, Snapchat, and Facebook while I pretended to be interested in the gray, ice-frosted neighborhoods and the skeleton trees floating past. It took everything in me not to start crying.

The bus groaned to a stop a few blocks from my house. "All ashore going to shore!" Larry the Toothless Bus Driver called out.

I dashed out into the cold and ran all the way home, past the stupid inflatable polar bear on my neighbor's lawn. I unlocked the door and walked inside.

Normally, I like having the house to myself after school since my mom and dad both work late. But today, the house was so quiet it felt like I was wearing soundproof headphones. I blasted a dance party mix to fill the eerie silence as I fetched a huge container of Morton Salt from the kitchen and went around to every drain I could find to pour in a huge heaping of Sleeknatch-sizzling salt.

"When I need to monster-proof my house, I use Morton Salt," I said in a cheesy commercial–actor's voice.

I even poured a salt circle around the outside of my

entire house. The neighbors must've thought I'd gone insane.

Then I did exactly as Vee instructed. I made myself a light snack and sat down to do my homework like a responsible human. Mom and Dad would have been so proud. I snapped a selfie and sent it to them, just so they could rest assured their wonderful daughter was happily at home, doing as she was told.

My phone rang with a number I didn't recognize. I took a gamble and answered it because, hey, I live on the edge.

"Kelly? It's Dawn Harker. Sorry to call you directly, but it's kind of an emergency. What are you doing right-right-right now?"

Let the record show that I, Kelly Ferguson, tried to have a single normal afternoon.

Really, I did.

16

Theo's mom only needs me for just one hour, I thought. *And if she needs me, then I have to protect the turtle hatchling. I can help her out and be back here before Mom and Dad get home. Easy peasy.*

I checked my book bag's inventory. Jump rope net. Check. Silver dagger. Check. *A Babysitter's Guide to Monster Hunting.* Double check. My unfinished book report that I had every intention of finishing. Checkity-check.

Found another Morton Salt container. Found a can of Raid under the kitchen sink. I grabbed it just in case and shuddered at the thought of having to use it.

Mama Vee is going to be so peeved I went on a

job without her permission. Let her be peeved! I'm almost a grown-up. I can handle this.

I chugged the cold coffee my parents had left in the pot that morning. It was thick and sludgy, and it made my heart race and my brain yell "Go time!"

Bzzt. Bzzt. Dawn texted me:

I'm outside!

Coming!

I zipped up my arsenal and skipped outside. I was actually happy to see Dawn.

A small green Ford that was missing a hubcap pulled into the driveway.

"Yo! Yo!" Dawn called out. "Thank you so much, Kelly! You have no idea how much this means to me," she said, putting her hand to her heart. Under her parka, I saw that she was wearing a black Olive Garden uniform. "My boss thinks I'm on my break."

"My parents think I'm doing homework," I said. "Hey, Theo!"

In the back, Theo was buckled into his rear-facing car seat. A mirror attached to the back seat's headrest let us see his adorable, toothless smile. As Dawn drove out of my neighborhood, Theo's little legs gleefully kicked the air. Cartoony green turtles were printed on his pajamas.

"Cute jammies," I said nervously.

"I wasn't going to call you, but then I thought I should just call you. And in case you couldn't tell, I can't exactly afford a full-time nanny at the moment."

"My pleasure. How's he doing?"

Dawn wiped her hand across her forehead. "Yeah, he's good," she said, licking her lips. I saw her cheeks were sunken and pale. Her hair was slicked with sweat. "Me, however. I've been better."

Last night Dawn looked young and healthy. Today she was weak and thin.

"Yikes. Do you have the flu?"

She shrugged and squinted at the road. Even her hands seemed pallid, almost blue. "I dunno what I have. Something's coming over me. . . . I can feel it crawling up the back of my skull like . . . brain freeze or something. . . . I just know we gotta go somewhere . . . ," she trailed off.

"The doctor?" I said. "Whatever you need."

"No. Not there. I've been having weird daydreams all afternoon," she mumbled.

Her head wobbled as she strained to see the rushing road ahead of her.

"I wish Frank was here. We were such a good team."

She turned the wheel suddenly, and we veered into oncoming traffic.

"Dawn!" I screamed, reaching for the wheel.

A truck shot toward us as she turned down a street. Theo began to wail.

"It's okay, honey," Dawn said, eerily calm.

"Dawn, I think you should pull over."

"I'm fine," she said, her voice getting woozy.

Something was wrong with her neck. At first I thought there was some kind of infection on it, but then I reached over and pulled back her jacket collar and saw two throbbing blue-black bite marks on her jugular.

I shivered. Some kind of bug had bit her.

"Dawn, I don't think you should be driving."

She sped up. The tiny car shook.

In his car seat, Theo shrieked.

"It's okay, Theo. She told me to go this way," she said slowly.

"Who told you? Dawn! Please! You're scaring Theo and me!"

"Hi, sweetie. Mommy loves you," said Dawn, waving in the rearview mirror.

We shot past a beach access sign. The small car bounced toward the dunes. I reached over to pull the hand brake, but Dawn snatched my arm.

"You can't take him!" she screamed at me. "He's mine!"

The Ford smashed up a hill covered in seagrass. In a spray of sand, we raced down the shore toward a long, narrow wooden pier over the water. A fisherman casting his line over the ledge spat out his cigar and jumped over the wooden railing just as the car rolled over his fish bucket. I reached over and tried to press down on the brakes with my hands, but Dawn kicked me.

"This is what I'm supposed to do!" she wailed.

At the very edge of the wooden pier, Dawn slammed on the brakes.

Dawn had a glazed, sleepy look in her eyes. "We're here."

She scratched the weeping bites on her neck. I didn't want to spend another second in the car, but the pier was so narrow the car barely fit on it, and the doors would only open an inch. I couldn't squeeze out. We were trapped inside, facing the endless black ocean.

Waves smashed. The old wooden boardwalk groaned below us. There was a shimmy. A crack. The car shifted and moved forward. I needed to get Theo out of there. I climbed over to the back seat to unbuckle him. Theo kicked and wailed.

The baby wasn't crying. He was warning me.

A powerful thumping rose behind us. Thundering footsteps.

"Here comes Bullgarth," Dawn said with a dewy smile.

"Bull who?!"

I followed Dawn's gaze, and my stomach filled with cold terror. The beast she called Bullgarth was charging down the dock on all fours like an angry, mutated silverback gorilla. It was the monster from last night. His huge paws shuddered the wooden boards. His twisted horns lowered, aiming right for us.

I covered Theo with my body as glass exploded. Monster bone shrieked against metal as the car skidded toward the edge of the dock. I tried to unbuckle Theo from his car seat, but his legs were stuck in the straps.

"Dawn, help!" I cried.

"It's okay, Kelly," she said matter-of-factly. "He's only here for the baby."

The monster snarled through the shattered rear window and tore the back door off, hurling it into the ocean, like he was skipping stones on a Sunday.

I reached for Theo, but Bullgarth's hairy paws ripped the entire car seat from its base.

"No! Get away!" I screamed.

I gasped as the monster shook the car seat upside down. The baby dropped into the beast's giant, padded palm.

Bullgarth unleashed a throaty roar in my face. I recoiled, petrified.

Crick-crack!

The front of the car jolted down.

Wooden boards fell away beneath us. Cradling the

baby against his chest, the ape-man monster backed away as the creaky dock collapsed into the sea.

"Bye-bye, Kelly," Dawn said with eerie calm.

I clambered over to Dawn and undid her seat belt as the car tipped forward. I pulled her by the jacket toward the ripped-open door.

Through the windshield, the gloomy ocean came into full view. I was still struggling to pull Dawn out of the car when it plunged into the icy waters.

A meaty paw caught my arm, catching me in mid-air. A giant splash swallowed the Ford. I watched the car sink into the merciless sea.

Bullgarth's curious, glistening silver eyes studied me as I dangled helplessly in his grasp. It took me a second to realize, the beast had saved us. Maybe he wanted a snack for later.

He lifted Dawn and me onto the cracked ledge. Baby Theo fidgeted in the monster's other arm, pulling little fistfuls of brown fur. I grew very still, not wanting to spook Bullgarth.

"Please. Don't hurt him. Just . . . give him to me," I said, my voice trembling.

I slowly held out my hands. Fur-Face glanced from me to the baby.

"It's okay, Kelly," Dawn said beside me with a dazed smile. "He's not going to hurt him. Go on, Bullgarth. Take him."

"No. Don't listen to her, Bullgarth. She doesn't know what she's talking about," I pleaded.

The monster flared his large, wet nostrils and howled as he raced off with the child.

A wail came from above. Looking up, I saw a blur of brown climbing a telephone pole on the shoulder of Sutton Beach Road. Bullgarth swung along the wires like a trapeze artist. I choked. The baby was being held in the monster's orangutan-like feet, bobbling along in the grip of his toes.

"That is so dangerous, Bullgarth!" I screamed, running underneath them. "Do not do that! Bad Bullgarth! Bad!"

The powerful creature launched from a wire and took the baby in his arms, just before he slammed down on the roof of a seaside tourist shop that was closed for the winter.

Whoa.

I scurried after them as Bullgarth roared down at me and then leaped from the roof of the Surf Shack to the roof of Seashelly's Swim Gear to the roof of Pappy's Fish Fry. I grabbed the jump rope from my book bag and charged forward, tying one end into a loop.

Remember Heck Weekend. Weapons training. Aiming the rope is all about timing. Wait for it, Kelly. You gotta get this right.

I released the spinning jump rope. It flew high and lassoed the beast's twisting horns. I hung on to the handle and was taken for a monster sleigh ride across the empty parking lot. The ground punched my ribs. Bullgarth shook his giant head and swung me into the side of a dumpster with a clang. Still, I held on tight.

Bullgarth howled and charged across the street and into an overgrown cemetery. Tall grass whipped into my face as I dodged two-hundred-year-old graves. His giant feet crushed slate gravestones like they were snail shells.

I flung myself around the base of a towering, angelic statue and wrapped the jump rope around its heavy base.

The beast's horns jerked back. His ginormous feet flew out from underneath him, and the ground shook when his big fuzzy butt slammed into it. Baby Theo thumped onto Bullgarth's chest and rolled onto the long, soft grass, just out of his reach.

The furry giant thrashed and snarled, but he was tethered to the angel statue.

"Not so fast, Hairy Pants."

I picked up Theo and kissed his head. I wiped the scraggily hairs and bits of leaves from his turtle pajamas. He needed a diaper change and a bath, pronto.

"You better not have given him fleas," I said, cuddling the poor baby.

With a heaving breath, the creature thrashed. The strong jump rope held him.

The sun had vanished into dishwater-colored twilight. We were all alone in the cold, forgotten cemetery that was more overgrown weeds and gnarly trees than graves. The people buried here were so ancient that no one had visited them in a hundred years.

I glared at Bullgarth. This beast was going to pay. I sat the baby on the ground, reached into my backpack, and removed the dagger.

The knife was heavy, thick. The enchanting green stone winked in the hilt. It electrified my arm with unstoppable power.

"Don't look, Theo," I said.

The monster saw me lifting the knife, and his stormy eyes bulged in terror. His long, donkey-like ears drooped, and his lower lip quivered over his tusks.

"Sorry, Bullgarth. You seem like a nice monster, but I can't let you get away with this."

I noticed the fur around his neck was thinning and patchy, as if it had been rubbed off. There were scars on his wrists from what looked to be shackles. Someone had chained this guy up. Maybe it was an escaped circus freak, or maybe it was part of some black-market monster smuggling trade gone bad. Or maybe Bullgarth was the victim of a cruel, evil bully.

I heard a gurgle from the ground. Theo was staring at me with those big blue eyes. I know this is going to sound weird, but something in that baby's gaze told me not to do it.

I glanced at the ugly beast and lowered the dagger.

"Go and tell your friends to leave us alone."

Bullgarth's sagging ears perked up. He was happy I was letting him live.

I bent down to scoop up the baby. Then I heard the jump rope snap. Bullgarth was loose.

Looking up, I saw that his sweet puppy-dog expression had turned to fury.

He was going to eat me.

The grind of a motorcycle engine zipped toward us.

Thweep! Thweep!

Bullgarth stumbled as a barrage of red darts impaled his fur. Bullgarth wildly swatted at them, but his jaw went slack and his eyes rolled back into his head. He made a confused grunt, and I jumped out of the way as he fell face forward.

The dirt bike skidded to a stop. Black boots kicked down the stand. Lowering a blowgun, Liz LeRue smirked at me.

"You never learn, do you, newb?"

18

" I thought you were in Tennessee!" I said.

"That's what I wanted everyone to think," Liz said.

I helped her bind the unconscious, eight-foot-tall hairy monster's arms and legs with a glimmering golden rope.

"I was staying in a tent behind the willow tree at the end of your block the whole time. After Madame Moon's warning, I wasn't taken any chances."

My mouth hung open. Liz shook her head, amused.

"The hunter has become the hunted," she said, casually texting someone. "I'm so proud of you, Ferguson!"

One thing I had learned about Liz, the more danger I was in, the happier she seemed to be.

"I had a hunch Serena was coming to town, so I faked going AWOL. That way I could do my thing and not get caught by her or one of her hairy goons. I wasn't exactly planning on blowing my cover so early, but it seemed like you needed the help."

I stared at my crazy friend with deep admiration. I thought she had abandoned me, but she had actually been looking out for me the whole time. I threw my arms around her, and she instantly shoved me away.

"Easy, sparky. I have a bad feeling the dumb ape's just the first of many. Thanks for drawing this ugly mutt out, though."

"Wait a second," I said. "You were using me as bait?"

Liz shrugged.

"Stop using me as bait, Liz!"

"But you're so good at it," she said, patting me on the head.

It grew dark as I explained to Liz that Berna, Curtis, and Cassie were tracking down a mansion where Serena might be hiding. Headlights swept the gravestones. The babysitter mobile chugged into view. Wugnot hopped out, adjusting his "We're #1" trucker hat around his nubby horn. The hobgoblin scowled at Liz.

"Think you're pretty smart, doncha?" Wugnot grumbled. "Had me driving around in circles."

Liz tapped her temple. "All part of the plan, Wuggie."

Wugnot shot a snot rocket at her. His tail pointed at me. "Vee told you to stay home."

I was about to explain myself when the squashy hobgoblin tossed me a diaper bag and an emergency bottle of formula.

"Save it for the judge," he said. "Brought you some wipes and dipes. Well, aren't you a handsome widdle man?" Wugnot said in a surprisingly silly tone of voice.

No one is immune to the power of a cute baby, not even an ex–man-eating troll.

Baby Theo reached out and yanked on the gold ring hanging from the hobgoblin's warty snout. Wugnot giggled and pried Theo's fingers from his nose.

As I fed and changed Theo on the front seat of the babysitter mobile, Wugnot and Liz hooked a motorized cable to the rope tied around Bullgarth and slowly reeled the enormous, snoozing beast into the back of the van.

"Should've turned this thing into a fur coat when you had the chance," Liz said.

I didn't want to tell Liz about the sad look I saw in Bullgarth's eyes or the strange connection I felt to the dangerous beast. She would call me soft.

Wugnot buckled Theo into a baby seat in the van and we headed for the beach.

Red and blue lights washed over the crumbling dock. Yellow "Do Not Cross" tape was already strung across the scene. We slowed to a crawl near the sandy dunes, just out of sight of the police cars and fire trucks. A Coast Guard boat was patrolling the waters, shining spotlights on Dawn's sinking car.

"Officer Muntz," Liz whispered, nodding toward a policeman with profound cheekbones. "Not my biggest fan."

"Where's Dawn?" I whispered to Liz.

Liz crept out of the van and into the cold seagrass. She found Dawn unconscious, hidden among the tall reeds. There was a red dart in Dawn's chest. I shot a "how could you?" look at Liz. She shrugged.

"It was for her own safety," Liz said. "We'll fix her up back at HQ."

We quickly carried Dawn's limp body into the front seat of the van, propped her up, and buckled her in.

As we drove onto the highway toward babysitter HQ, Bullgarth stirred in his sleep.

I snapped a selfie with him and sent it to Berna with a message:

Monsters: 0, Babysitters: 1

19

Liz leaned her dirt bike against the stone lion of our chapter HQ. We carried Dawn inside. Berna wheeled a gurney down the hall.

I cradled Baby Theo's head in my hand. "Something bad bit her neck."

Berna pulled on blue latex gloves and softly turned Dawn's head to the side. The centers of the two bumps on her neck had turned black, with dark ropy veins spreading underneath them.

Berna took a sharp breath.

Please don't say it was spiders. Please don't say it was spiders. I really don't want to go hunt spiders.

"Looks like a spider bite," Berna said.

I winced.

Berna whirled the gurney past the training room, the library, and into the laboratory. I briskly walked beside her, holding Theo.

"Dawn was acting crazy," I said quickly. "She wasn't herself. So that means whatever spider bit her had—what's the word? Nuero? Neurotic?"

"Neurotoxins," Berna said. "Means poisons that affect the brain."

"That's the one," I said.

"I'll have to draw some blood, run some tests."

"Can you do that?"

"Kelly, I've been studying to be a doctor since I was eight."

"Yeah, but you're, like, thirteen."

"Actually, I'm twelve. I've done only minor surgery."

"Berna, I'm starting to feel very jealous of how smart you are."

"Don't be. It's the result of a lifetime of pressure from my mother."

I followed her to the center of the laboratory and flicked on the buzzing, bright lights. "Your mom encourages you to do minor surgery?"

"She was a babysitter," she said, scrubbing up. "She gets it."

"No way! Was she with the Rhode Island chapter?"

"Focus. I'll give Dawn a minor sedative so she can rest while we figure out what she's infected with.

There's no telling what state she's going to be in when she wakes up, so we have to figure out an antidote for her right away."

She opened a metal box where ten thin, long needles shined brightly. "Wanna help?"

"Gaaaah" was all I could manage to say as I turned away, woozy.

I had stared down the mouths of sea monsters, werewolves, and nightmares, but it was the sight of a slender hypodermic needle that turned me into jelly.

"I, uh, I think I'm going to salt the house to keep out the Sleeknatch," I said as I backed toward the door. "Rock on, Dr. Vincent."

In the kitchen, I found a large, half-empty bag of rock salt. As I poured it down every drain in HQ, I heard the quick slapping of bare feet on marble. Mama Vee stalked toward me, pulling her silver Rapunzel hair into a crooked bun. A thick line appeared in between her scrunched eyebrows.

"Vee, before you say anything," I said, putting up my hands, "just know that I thought it was just going to be for an hour."

"You were supposed to go home and rest. I don't tell you to do things because I like telling you what to do. I do them for your own safety."

"I hear you and I am sorry. But if you're so worried about me, why'd you assign me to babysit Theo in the first place? You claim I'm not a sitter, and yet, you give me a newborn? Why couldn't you have picked Berna? She's clearly the smartest one here."

"The Mighty Kang didn't tell Berna about the turtle hatchling. It told you and only you."

"What's so special about him?"

Shadows darkened in the room as Vee looked down at Baby Theo.

"Sitters from way back foretold of a childminder, a warrior, who would one day rise up to destroy the Boogeypeople," she said. "They claimed the warrior would be born under the Sword of the Sitter. A constellation in the shape of a sword.

"The Sword of the Sitter appeared in the sky the night this little love was born."

I cocked my head to the side and studied the little

boy with his gummy smile.

"This adorable mush is going to save the world?"

"He's too young to show his powers yet. But one day, I have a feeling he's going to shine."

I gently touched the little chunk's cheek, hoping I was strong enough to protect him.

"You help Liz with the beast. I'll give this beautiful mister a baff! Would you like that? Yeah you would! We'll go have quick bafftime and a bot-bot give you nap-nap. Okaaaay, little turtle wurtle? And don't worry about Mommy. We'll take good care of her. I promise with all my heart. Yes we will. We will!"

Vee wandered off, bobbling Theo in her arms. Apart from being a great monster hunter, she was such a pro. I caught up with Liz and Wugnot as they pushed a large cage with Bullgarth still sleeping inside it into a freight elevator at the end of the hall.

"Berna's running a blood test, so don't go into the lab," I said to Wugnot.

The hobgoblin ran his meaty paw over his mouth and smacked his lips. "Thanks for the heads-up."

Wugnot used to be a *Hominemque comedere*—an eater of men—but he quit cold turkey eight years ago (if you don't count his relapse). But we all knew he could flip out if he got around fresh blood.

We descended in the elevator with the caged beast.

"Have you guys heard from Cassie or Curtis?" I asked.

"They're checking out another mansion before heading here," Wugnot said. "Hargrave Manor. I think Cass was happy to get rid of me so she could have time alone with Curtis."

Hargrave Manor. Why does that sound familiar?

I gasped when I remembered the old rhyme kids said about Harriet Hargrave, the infamous sixteen-year-old girl who killed her family with hedge clippers:

Harriet Hargrave, child, what did you do?
Snipped and clipped your family in two.
Did you mistake your parents for a hedge?
What evil thing sent you over the edge?
Harriet Hargrave, what else will you do?
Say her name three times, and she'll come for YOU.

I sent Cassie and Curtis a quick group text.

> You guys close?

No response.

The elevator descended into the dank, stone-cold basement of the cottage. We wheeled Bullgarth under the old brick archways where gleaming brass nameplates were stuck to the walls. "Agatha Barnes, 1763–1779." "Thomas Brattle 1769–1799." I shivered. The bones of the founding chapter of the Rhode Island order were all buried down here.

Chains jangled from around the corner. The snapping of a metal collar. I rushed into the corner of the basement where Wugnot and Liz were attempting to chain Bullgarth through the bars.

"No chains!" I said.

"Are you crazy?" Liz said.

Bullgarth rose with a growing howl and crunched his head against the top of the cage. He grumbled and rubbed the lump on top of his head.

I pointed to a ring of red, raw skin under the patches of rubbed-off fur around Bullgarth's neck. "I think he gets locked up a lot."

"Because he's a wild monster," said Liz. "And I don't care if I have to wax the fur off his hairy butt cheeks,

128

this thing is going to give me answers about Serena and Kevin."

The Sasquatch-thing looked up suddenly.

"You can understand me, can't you?" Liz shouted at him.

Bullgarth wrung his hairy paws together, considering whether or not he should answer the question.

"Grunt once for yes, twice for no."

He tilted his horned head down, crouching so he could peer directly at Liz. Liz kicked the bars. Bullgarth didn't startle. He just stared at Liz.

"Quit looking at me, freak!" Liz shouted again.

His enormous claws scratched at the worn fur around his collar, but the beast's silver eyes never once left Liz.

I dug my hand into my backpack. "Liz, he left me this."

Liz stopped. Her entire being focused on the small, dented, scratched tin soldier in the palm of my hand. She slowly turned the pewter figurine upside down to look under its base. A quiet, shocked noise caught in her throat.

"This was my brother's," she said in a hushed tone.

Bullgarth sighed a deep sort of purring sigh.

She showed me the bottom of the soldier. Underneath all the scratch marks were two small crooked letters that I hadn't noticed until this very moment (I blame the poor penmanship): "KL."

Kevin LeRue.

"Where did you get this?" Liz said, her voice trembling.

Her shaking fist clutched the tin toy. She smashed her knuckles into the iron bars.

"What have you done with Kevin, you—you—stupid shag rug!"

Bullgarth tapped his chest and made deep breathy huffs. His glimmering eyes softened.

"TELL ME!" Liz demanded.

Frustrated, the bigfoot slammed his fist into his chest. His sad, powerful moan was full of yearning, longing. It sounded almost human.

His rumbling roar stopped Liz. She leaned forward with curious wonder.

"What'd that thing say?" Wugnot whispered to me.

I couldn't answer. I was too excited and afraid.

The beast reached his giant hand out through the bars. Transfixed, Liz made no move to step away or protect herself as his paw, twice the size of her face, gently touched the side of her cheek.

Tail twitching anxiously, Wugnot took a protective step forward, but I put my hand on his shoulder. We stood totally still as the monster's paw rose slowly up Liz's face and wiped the tears that were falling from her eyes. His own tears had slicked the fur around his cheeks into dark stripes.

Liz choked. She could barely form a whisper.

"Kevin? Is that you?"

The beast's eyes brightened. His lips curled into a tusky smile as he nodded. Liz held the giant's warm, hairy paw through the bars.

"No way," I said in hushed wonder.

"Come closer," Liz demanded. "Let me see your right eyebrow."

The monster pulled back the fur from his forehead, showing a tiny scar just above his right eyebrow. Liz gasped.

"When Kevin was four, he fell and cut open his right eyebrow. . . . That's the scar!"

She quickly unlocked the side of the cage.

"Wouldn't do that," Wugnot warned.

Liz boldly entered the monster's pen.

"Liz! It could be a trap!" Wugnot shouted.

But Liz was only listening to the voice of her broken heart. She had been waiting almost a decade to see her brother again. Nothing was going to stop her.

Bullgarth charged suddenly and embraced her with his woolly arms. Clinging tightly, Liz was almost buried under his waves of long, matted fur.

"I never stopped looking for you," she said quietly.

Kevin, the monster once known to us as Bullgarth, held his sister tightly. He wailed long and low as his massive paw stroked her pink-and-black hair.

Wugnot and I stood outside the bars. I wiped the back of my sleeve across my eyes. I heard a snotty snuffle and saw Wugnot flick a green tear from the corner of his eye just before he pulled the brim of his hat down low.

"How is this possible?" I said.

Liz studied Kevin's face. She traced her finger across

his black snout, his dagger-sized tusks, his flea-infested fur.

"She turned him. Somehow. She took him and she turned him," Liz whispered.

Kevin nodded sadly. She carefully touched the jagged edge of his broken horn. He winced and pulled away.

A wrenching growl from Kevin's stomach broke the emotional moment.

"You hungry, little brother?"

Monster Kevin patted his furry stomach.

Liz led him out of the cage. "Let's get you something to eat."

"I don't think you should take him out of there," Wugnot suggested as Liz led Kevin from the cage. "It's going to be all hugs and cuddles and then screaming and running. Fine. Don't listen to me. I'm just a monster. What do I know?"

"The Spider Queen did this to you?" Liz asked.

Kevin nodded.

"Is she here?" Liz handed him a piece of paper and a pencil.

With fear in his eyes, he nodded again. It sent snowballs rolling down my spine. "That was nine years ago," I said. "That would make you . . . fourteen. Around my age."

Kevin nodded. I couldn't help but feel terrible for the little boy who grew up imprisoned in the body of a beast, forced to serve Queen Serena's awful whims.

"Is this her house?" I said, pointing at a drawing he had made for us.

He nodded quickly, excited to be understood. He

jammed his pencil down and drew lines across the house. They looked like prison bars. The point on the pencil snapped. Kevin dragged it across the page, ripping through the paper. Roaring, he swept the whole thing away and buried his gorilla face in his hands.

Liz gently patted his heaving, scraggly mane. "It's okay, Kev."

He leaned his giant horned head on Liz's shoulder.

"Where is this house?" I asked.

He went quiet. He couldn't tell. He musn't tell. He touched the chain marks around his neck and wrists.

"She can't hurt you anymore," Liz said. "You're with me now, little bro."

The beast gave his sister a thankful expression. His paws crawled in the air like vicious spiders, as if he was trying to tell us *No matter what you do, Serena the Spider Queen cannot be beaten.*

"Tell us where she's hiding so I can go there and clean out her hive for good, and she'll never hurt you again," said Liz.

"Hargrave Manor?" I asked. "Is that it?"

Kevin looked at me, shocked.

"That's where Cassie and Curtis went!" I exclaimed.

"Human heart stew!" Wugnot ladled a steaming bowl of stew out of the kitchen cauldron and slid it before Kevin. "Minus the human heart, of course. Extra spicy. Old hobgoblin recipe. It'll put hair on your chest. Not that you need it."

Kevin picked up the bowl with one paw and gulped the food down like a high school hipster shooting a single shot of espresso at a poetry slam. Wugnot went to pour more into the bowl when Kevin picked up the cast-iron cauldron by the handle and guzzled the remaining stew.

"Hey! I was gonna have some of that," Wugnot said, sadly looking at the soup ladle in his hand.

Kevin's hairy arm wiped the slobber from his long, dark beard. He belched a gust of reeking wind that hung in the air like a methane gas leak, and then ambled over to the fridge.

"Don't let him near that fridge!" whined Wugnot. "We're not gonna have anything left for Christmas dinner!"

"He's had a terrible life," Liz said, sounding warm and kind, unlike her usual acidic tone. "How can I say no to him?"

"You ever babysit a Squatch?" Wugnot said. "They're impossible."

"We're the greatest babysitters who ever lived," Liz announced. "We can look after him. Think of it like a mission from your clandestine hobgoblin days."

"Yeah!" I said, and high-fived Liz.

I stupidly held up my hand to Kevin for a high five. His paw slammed into my palm, and I went flying backward.

Kevin walked around in circles and squatted down in the corner.

"He better not be doing what I think he's doing," Wugnot said.

The beast was, in fact, doing what Wugnot thought he was doing.

Nasty!

Kevin finished his business and kicked his feet backward like a dog covering his poo with leaves.

"You're cleaning that up," Wugnot said, pointing at Liz.

Suddenly, Kevin straightened up. His wet snout

sniffed the air. He shoved Liz aside and bounded out of the kitchen and into the hallway. His galloping paws slipped across the floor and he slid, bumping into an aquarium full of snails. The glass box toppled, and Wugnot dove, barely able to catch it.

"Stop that ape!" Wugnot shouted.

Liz and I dashed around a corner, trying to keep up with the hairy streak in front of us.

Kevin swung open a door, and we saw just what he smelled: Baby Theo.

Mama Vee was giving him a bath in a giant claw-foot tub.

Theo stopped splashing. He started to cry, sensing trouble darkening the doorway.

"It's okay! He's my brother!" Liz cried out.

Kevin howled and lunged into the room, paws out for the baby in the bath. Mama Vee spun Theo out of the water, cradling his naked butt in her arms while kicking over the tub. Steaming water sluiced the floor, distracting the giant for a moment as Berna rounded the corner, raising a baby rattle in her hand.

"Hey, dog boy!"

Berna aimed the rattle at the monster's forehead.

"No!" Liz screamed as the end of the rattle exploded.

A capsule of purple mist exploded from the baby rattle and wound itself around the beast's face in erratic circles, as if it were a balloon with the air being let out. A giant sneeze sent the cotton candy–like cloud into fizzling bits. Kevin released a woozy wail, and his silver eyes crossed. He yawned and stumbled onto his butt, splashing in the tub water.

"Flumorian Flatulence Pellets," Berna said. "No fun to collect, but they have a powerful calming effect."

We watched the oversized ball of fur playing with the soap bubbles. Vee caught her breath. She was holding a knife she kept hidden inside her long braid for emergency situations.

"That's my brother, you idiot!" Liz screamed at Berna.

"Don't yell at me. He was about to eat Theo," Berna said.

"He was not!"

"Kinda was," said Wugnot.

Vee studied the dazed creature. "He must have been injected with some form of simian mutagen."

"I'd love to run some tests," Berna said.

"You're not poking my brother with a bunch of needles!" Liz said. "He's fine the way he is."

Everyone exchanged skeptical glances. Someone had to break the news to Liz.

"Liz, Dawn told me Kevin came to take Theo. Kevin was going to bring him to Serena."

Liz clenched her jaw. She didn't want to accept that maybe her brother was not a 100 percent nice kid.

"Liz, your brother's a monster and that's *cool*," Mama Vee said. "But . . . we have to be aware of the fact that, well, he's been gone a long time. There's no telling what kind of influence Serena or his captors have had on him throughout the years."

"You calling my brother a creep?"

"I'm saying that Kevin has been a monster longer than he's been a human," she said.

Liz rubbed her eyes. She was on the verge of tears.

I took Theo and put a clean diaper on him. "Kevin's

okay. He saved Dawn and me. So, I know there's good in him. Somewhere like deep, deep, deep down."

Liz looked at me thankfully.

Or is he like a Trojan horse sent by Serena? We didn't find Kevin. He found us. He could be a pawn in her bigger plan. . . .

"But," I continued cautiously, knowing Liz was not going to like what I had to say next, "I don't trust him around the baby. And it's my job to protect Theo."

"And it's my job to protect my brother," Liz said, baring her teeth.

I saw her fists coil up.

"I don't want a fight. Just keep him away from Theo," I said, snapping the buttons on the Theo's fresh jammies.

Mama Vee put it bluntly to Liz. "You want to keep Kevin, you have to train him."

Liz scowled. "Kevin's not a dog!"

"Smells like one," Wugnot snorted.

"Like you're one to talk, cheese-claws," said Liz, jabbing her finger at Wugnot.

"Careful where you point that digit, LeRue." Wugnot clicked his teeth at her and stormed out of the room.

"Like it or not, Liz, Kevin is a wild thing," Mama Vee said. "And we need to proceed with extreme caution."

Liz let out a humorless laugh. "I can't believe you

clowns. I finally find my brother, and you're acting like the best day of my life is the worst thing in the world." She took Kevin by the paw. "Come on, Kev. Let's ditch these losers. You can crash in my room."

Kevin wobbled to his feet and strummed his paws in the air, waving good-bye to all of us.

"Careful! Flumorian Flatulence wears off pretty quick," Berna called after her.

We watched them go, sister and eight-foot-tall hairy brother.

"How's Dawn?" I asked Berna.

Berna held up a vial of blood and swished it around.

"I've never seen anything like the venom in her system."

A cold draft from the echoing hallways ran its fingers across my shoulders.

"It attacks the neural system. Makes people do whatever the parasite wants them to do. Makes them their puppet."

"Is there a cure?" I asked.

"I've tried the usual antivenom remedies: Soro antibotropicocrotalico. Aracmyn. Anti Latrodectus. Nothing works."

My heart sank into despair.

"I do have one idea. If I were able to get ahold of the source of the venom—or better yet, the venom itself—I might be able to make an antidote from it."

I gagged at the thought of trying to catch whatever spider had bitten Dawn. I checked my phone. No replies from Cassie or Curtis. But plenty of angry, worried messages from my mother.

Where are you, Kelly?

Call us! You said you would be home!

DINNER READY IN 30 MINUTES, YOUNG LADY. U BETTER B HERE.

father and I r worried. y aren't u calling?

My stomach clenched. I had a sinking, gross feeling that I was about to be in major trouble on the home front.

"I gotta call my folks before they go nuclear," I said.

"Tell them you'll be back in twenty minutes," Vee said. "Wugnot will drive you home. I'll go check out Hargrave Manor. See if I can find Cassie and Curtis."

"What about the turtle hatchling?" I asked, feeding Theo a bottle of formula.

"Until Dawn gets better, we can't have Theo and Monster Kev in the same house. That's just a disaster waiting to happen."

"Where are you going to take him?"

"Your house."

"Are you crazy?"

"A little. Let's go get you a stroller," she said.

I followed her to the bust of Joan of Arc. She twisted the statue's head, and a far wall rumbled and descended into the floor. We darted down the dark, hidden staircase into the weapons room. A giant, gleaming sword that looked like it weighed more than me hung on the wall beside a pair of tomahawks made from two giant fangs.

A cabinet was filled with beakers full of funky monster parts. Jars of fire juice collected from the tongue of the Jersey Devil. Bottles of knockout troll farts. Venomous spittle. Gorgon armpit hives. A ball of evil elf earwax.

We moved down rows of weapons made to resemble toys. A ballistic soccer ball. G.I. Joe action figures that doubled as nunchaku. A Hatchimals egg loaded with an actual wild monster inside, lying in wait to pounce on whoever opened it.

Vee wheeled a black-and-gray baby stroller from behind a rack of teddy bear bombs. Its handles were smooth and sleek. The large, nubby wheels were ready for any obstacle. If Batman had a baby, this would be his stroller of choice.

"I give you the latest in stroller tech: the Lone Wolf

Tactical Stroller, Series Five. Developed by the sitters in the Tokyo office. The L-Five is the finest in baby transpo and protection. Ideal for running and traveling over rough terrain. The padded handlebars, with a cup-and-phone holder that offers nine positions to create the perfect fit for sitters of all heights, conceal two swords here and here. And . . ."

She flipped open a secret panel on the handle. Different buttons glowed.

4WD

SHIELD

SMOKE

OIL

POWER

BOOST

"The L-Five comes complete with four-wheel drive, invisible shield, smoke screen, oil slick, and duel power boosters."

Vee twisted a handle, and a small engine below the stroller purred with a high-pitched whine. A headlight flipped up in the front, and running boards sprang out in the back.

"With baby and driver, the L-Five can reach speeds of up to thirty miles an hour for quick escapes as needed. Oh, and the cup holder doubles as a gear shift."

"Wicked!"

We sat Baby Theo in the seat, buckled him in, and pulled the straps tight. His chubby legs kicked, and he bounced up and down.

"He loves it," I said with a smile.

Vee clicked a remote key, and the headlamp and running boards slid back into place as the power shut down. "Engine's electric. At full blast it'll only last twenty minutes, so don't forget to charge the battery. There's also a voice command option, but that's in prototype phase."

She handed me the key. "Happy strolling."

Wugnot tore into my quiet neighborhood, blasting his favorite Norwegian Christmas heavy metal band, Dark Yule. Piles of dead leaves tumbled across the frosty asphalt. How was I going to break the news to my parents that I was bringing a six-month-old home to dinner?

"Your parents are good humans," Wugnot said. "If you gotta tell 'em everything, well, just break it to 'em slowly."

My heart shot into my feet. "You think I should tell my parents?"

"Just make sure they're sitting down when you do. Most parents faint when you tell them the truth. When they come to, they're usually pretty reasonable."

I gnawed on the end of my sleeve, queasily thinking of confronting my folks. They were going to be ticked. And what if Dawn didn't get better—*ever*? Would I have to raise Theo on my own? This was beginning to feel like instant adulthood, and I was not psyched.

Snow began to fall. White flakes against the black sky. As if the cold front had arrived directly over my roof. I shuddered and zipped up my jacket.

"Crazy how Liz was looking for her brother this whole time and he just showed up," I said, not wanting to get out of the car and face my parents.

"If you ask me, and no one ever does, I don't think it's a coincidence," Wugnot said.

"You think Serena planned this?"

With a troubled expression Wugnot unbuckled Theo from his car seat. "I'm just saying that I think that lady's spinning her web bigger than any of us can see."

I unfolded the Lone Wolf from the back of the van and sat Theo inside it as he chewed on his slobbery hand. Wugnot tucked Theo's elephant blanket around him and then hefted a huge duffel bag into my arms that nearly toppled me over. "Baby supplies. You'll need 'em."

The front light on my house flicked on. My heart jumped.

"I'm gonna head back to HQ before that beast tears

the place apart. Good luck with your folks."

Wugnot drove off with a salute as I quietly unlocked the front door.

The warm smell of dinner filled the air. My mom and dad were busy in the kitchen with their backs to me. I ninja-swooped the stroller behind them and rocketed into my room, shutting the door behind me. Safe.

"Okay, Theo, here's the deal," I whispered, opening the bag of baby supplies. "You stay here and be quiet, and I'll come get you after I break the news to my parents, okay? Just try to take a nap. You've had a big day. We'll have you back with your mommy in no time, I promise."

I unfolded a small portable sleeper and placed him inside it. I fished through the supply bag. Toys, teething rings, jars of baby food, a portable baby monitor. I turned on the camera and aimed it at Theo and then shoved the monitor into my jacket pocket. Yes, this was going to work.

"Aaaaaeeeeaaaah," Theo gurgled.

"Sshhhh, sssssh, bedtime," I said, rocking his small sleeper.

"Kelly? Is that you?" called my mother.

"Be right out!" I said, frantically swishing the sleeper back and forth.

Theo drifted off to dreamland, and I sprang from my room.

My mom and dad were waiting outside my door. Both of them had their arms crossed, and they were not happy.

"Wooo! Crazy day! Here, let me help. I'll set the table."

I breezed into the living room and found the table had already been meticulously set. Candles were burning. The good silverware was out, and there were four plates.

"I was home, but then I got a call and had to go out and help that poor woman I babysat for last night."

"I thought we agreed, no more babysitting for the week," my mother said.

"I know, and I'm very sorry, but hear me out— What's with the fancy dinner? It smells incredible."

"Your father made lamb chops and his special duck-fat roasted potatoes," my mother said proudly.

"Delicious!" I said.

"And your mother's making chocolate lava cake! Woo boy!"

"Wow. What's the occasion?"

"We're having company!" my dad said, dashing into the kitchen.

I followed them curiously into the kitchen. Sauce was splattered on the walls. Pots bubbled over. Bags of groceries were hastily spilled across the floor. My dad held out a huge knife. "I'll chop the carrots if you wash the lettuce. Deal? Deal!"

I hadn't seen my father this excited since the Patriots won the Super Bowl. My mother had a big smile on her face too. I thought it was more than a little weird that they weren't yelling at me for being out so late—and yes, I was going to tell them about the six-month-old currently napping in my room—but why ruin their good mood?

"It was a slow day at All for One," my dad said, slicing into the carrots. He was co-owner and mechanic at All for One Auto outside Providence. It was tough work. "I was changing the oil on old Gus Barton's Chevy, and he was telling me how the cold was making his sciatica act up and how he needed to move out of Rhode Island and retire to Florida for the millionth time when the most beautiful car I have ever seen drove right past us. I had to stop and stare, and even old Gus shut his yap, and together we just gawked at the thing. A 1937 Rolls-Royce Phantom Three. V12 engine. Jet-black. Dripping with chrome and curves and style. I felt like I was seeing a vision of heaven come right at me."

He dreamily waved his knife in the air. His love of cars was notorious. It was the reason he became a mechanic. But even this was over-the-top for him. I looked at my mother. She was grating cheese, beaming from my father's story.

"There was a driver behind the wheel. An actual chauffeur, Kells! Uniform and everything! Can you beat that?"

"Sure can't, Dad."

"And what does he do? He pulls into the garage and parks it right in front of me. He gets out, doesn't say a word, real serious. Sunglasses. And he opens the back door. And who should step out of the back seat? The most gorgeous woman I have ever seen in my life! Face to die for! Jewels like the kind you see in magazines. This long silky red dress. She looked like a movie star– No, better. Like royalty! She looked like royalty. A fairy-tale lady . . ."

The blood in my veins thumped faster.

"Like a queen," my mother said with an awed whisper.

My stomach dropped. My eyes darted around the house.

"She glided right up to me and said with this accent– Russian maybe, or German, or gosh, now that I think about it, maybe it was British–and she said, real slow, 'You look like the right man.'" My dad giggled. I felt ill. "She asked me to take a look at her car for her, and we got to talking and . . . I don't know what we talked about, but it seemed like we talked for hours and hours about everything. Life, death, love, family. She was the most captivating woman in the entire world."

I choked with the sudden urge to throw up. "Was her name Serena?"

A huge smile spread across his face. "How did you know?"

The doorbell rang.

24

I lunged for the door, snapped the dead bolt, and spun around to my parents.

"She's evil! You can't let her in here!"

"Don't be silly, Kelly," my mother said. "She's rich and famous. How can she be evil?"

My jaw dropped. My mother prided herself on not being vapid and superficial. Her heroes were Amelia Earhart, Jane Goodall, Eleanor Roosevelt, and Michelle Obama. She frequently reminded me life was about your heart and spirit and the good you leave behind, not the bling and the likes.

And then I saw my mother scratch the side of her neck.

"Let me see your neck," I said slowly.

My mother self-consciously lifted her collar to block the skin under her chin and ear. My dad pushed me aside. "Stop being rude, Kelly. We're lucky someone like Miss Von Kessell wants to dine with us."

My hand shot out and grabbed his wrist. My strength and speed shocked him and my mother.

"Kelly, let go of my hand," my father said. He was getting angry.

"Mom. Dad. I have something very important to tell you. There are monsters in the world. They're real. And I fight them. That's what I do when I go out baby-sitting. And now one of the biggest monsters of all is right outside our door."

"That's nice, dear," my mother said with a bizarre smile.

"We know that's what you do," my dad said. "It's fine with us."

"How do you know that?" I said.

"She told us."

As my father unlocked and then opened the door, I saw the veiny spider bite on his neck. A frightened gasp escaped my mouth. I ran toward my bedroom, but my mother stopped me. She was holding a kitchen knife at her side.

"Sit down, daughter."

All my training and studying for fighting monsters did not prepare me for the chilling, twisted look in my own mother's eyes. The skin on her neck was off-colored, drained. My brain seized up like an over-loaded computer.

"Come in, come in!" I heard my father say.

I slowly faced the front door. She wore large Gucci sunglasses. A diamond-encrusted hornet that must have cost a million dollars hung from her necklace. Her face glowed like a Snapchat filter in real life. Her hair was done up in elegant, tight braids that showed off her impossibly long, pale neck. Her silky white dress hugged her every curve. Tiny snowflakes dusted her hair, giving her an extra-glittery shine.

For a monster she looks fabulous.

She had not aged a day since her portrait was painted. Then I heard the enchanting voice with its unplaceable accent.

"What a dump," Serena said.

"Thank you!" said my father, bowing.

"Welcome to our humble home!" my mother said.

Serena's exotic eyes fixed upon me. I glanced down to see if she had spider legs, but all I could see were the flashes of two tall leather boots. Her heels clacked on the floor as she took long strides toward me. She seemed to float like she was headed up the red carpet.

"Very clever, salting your home to keep out my Sleeknatch. So I had to come and pay you a visit myself. I don't believe we've been properly introduced."

She offered me her hand. It sparkled with snake rings made of rose gold, and million-dollar bug-shaped bracelets.

"I know exactly who you are, Serena," I said, standing my ground.

"Then you'll know to bow before speaking to me," she said with a red-lipstick smile.

My fists curled up in defiance. I could feel my engine revving. Something twisted inside me, preparing to snap. I had to get ready to fight. Go into warrior-beast mode.

Be cool, Kelly. No sudden moves. You need to get the antidote from her to cure Dawn and your parents.

"Let my parents go," I said.

"But who else will serve us dinner? Peter. Alexa."

She snapped her fingers. My mother and father blinked for a moment.

"I'm sorry . . . who are you?" my mother said.

"Your queen, and you will do as I say."

My mother swooned, dizzy. She touched the side of her neck. Her spider bite was quivering, sickly.

"Don't listen to her, Mom! She's poisoned you!"

"Technically, my spiders poisoned her. Silly girl," sneered Serena.

With a lost expression my mother cocked her head strangely to the side.

"I'll just go check on supper, honey," my mother said as she scurried off into the kitchen. My dad followed. It broke my heart to see them grovel.

"Stop this," I said to Serena.

"Let's be civilized, Kelly. Even the Vikings had tea. Sit," she said, gliding into the dining room. She lowered herself into my father's chair at the head of the table.

I slid into the chair where my mother usually sat at the other end of the table. I reached for my phone on the table—

A gooey ribbon shot out, snapping my phone into Serena's grip. Her silky spiderweb retracted quickly into the back of her dress.

"No phones at the table," she said, looking at my phone. "What an amazing device. It's enslaved more children than all seven Boogeymen combined. I guess that's why they call it the web." She chuckled at her terrible pun. "Don't look so sad, child. I'm doing you a favor. If it weren't for me, your parents would be grounding you right now. But now, they're happy and will do whatever you want me to tell them to do. Go on. Try it."

"No!"

"Alexa, give Kelly her allowance."

"Kelly doesn't get an allowance," my mother said. "That's why she works so hard."

"Just shut up and give her all the money in your purse."

My mother staggered up to the table and dumped the contents of her purse before me. Serena rolled her eyes. "That's all you have in there? Pathetic. Shoo!"

I slipped my hand into my pocket and turned down the baby monitor so Serena couldn't hear Baby Theo. Did she know he was here? Were we playing a game?

If she wants to play, let's play. Remember your training. Defiance can be a weapon in itself.

Serena draped her purple-and-black spotted fur on the chair beside her. I swear I saw it move. Maybe it was still alive. She hooked her leather-bound leg over her knee and kicked her heel back and forth. "This is a very sad home you have here," she said, looking around. "I cannot believe you people chose to live like this."

"We can't all murder people for their money," I said.

Serena scowled, a dark fire in her eyes. She was not used to anyone talking back to her.

"Isn't that what babysitters do? For far less money, of course." She inspected her flawlessly painted black fingernails. "But I'm not here to talk about your poor lower-class life. I'm here to talk about your poor lower-class death."

"Lamb à la Peter!" My parents walked in with pots and dishes.

159

"Horrid," sneered Serena.

"You're welcome!" sang my mom. "It's not every day we get someone famous like you through town, isn't that right, Kells?"

I couldn't stand to see my mother like this.

I glared at Serena. "Please don't do this. They're my parents."

"And he was my brother!" she hissed. Teeth bared.

"Who are you talking about?" I said.

"The Grand Guignol"–Serena simmered, panting–"was my brother. And you killed him."

She was shaking. The buckles on her leather boots trembled.

I sat bolt upright. I had had no idea the Boogeyperson I vanquished on Halloween was this monster's brother.

Serena screamed, and her eyelids closed and fluttered like furious bat wings. "And now I am going to watch you suffer for what you did to my little Guignolly!"

Her little Guignolly? She was talking about the dreaded demon that tried to roast me alive as if he were a sweet, innocent child. Maybe to her, he still was.

"Look. I'm real sorry, I didn't know he was your brother. But he was hurting kids, and that breaks rule number one in my guide," I said, my voice shaking.

160

Serena settled herself. She fixed the black brooch in her hair, and its claws clamped down on her braids, as if it were alive. I squinted and saw that the thing in her hair *was* alive. It was a spider.

She uses a spider like a hair clip. I might vomit.

"My brother's only fault was that he was a dreamer," she said with a self-righteous smirk. "Whoever heard of an army of nightmares taking over the world? I warned him, but he was shortsighted. And he never listened to me. That is not how things are done."

Her nails clacked on a dinner plate.

"To help monsters, we need to rid the world of the one thing that has always been in our way: babysitters."

She smiled at me, and fangs lowered from her red gums.

"It's simple, really. Kill the babysitters, and we'll thrive. And I'd like to start with you."

She pointed her black fingernail at me. A gold scorpion bracelet wrapped around her wrist clicked its stinger threateningly.

"You scored major points with the babysitters of the world when you killed my brother, Kelly Ferguson. Now all those downtrodden nannies and that old decrepit council of gray-haired sitters who adore you, their youngling hero, will watch as you destroy the organization from the inside."

My heart jumped. The babysitter council considered me to be a youngling hero? Serena had to be lying. I couldn't even pass the training exam. But I needed to focus. This witch was talking about killing the babysitters.

"So just think of how crushing it will be to the Queen governess when she hears that her beloved beacon of hope has turned into a monster. They might have high hopes for you, but I do not. Just look at you. You're low-rent."

I leaned back, stung.

"I've done my homework on you, Kelly Ferguson. Straight-A student. Yearbook editor. Mathlete. Murderer." She clacked her nails at me, as if to sum up my entire existence with a small flick.

I swallowed.

"I see you, Kelly. Your messy hair. Your dirty jeans. Your untied shoelaces. You could be a rose, but instead you choose to be a bud."

She tilted her head, her gaze digging into my soul.

"I see that look in your eyes. I've seen it in so many other frightened children as they stare upon the future and see the abyss of adulthood rolling toward them, swallowing them in its misery. Well, you're not ready for it. You're not good enough. You're not strong enough. You are just a weak little child."

My throat clenched up. She saw my hurt expression,

and it filled her with glee.

"I can change that. I can make you stronger than you could possibly imagine."

My eyes widened with horrified curiosity.

My mother poured Serena a glass of red wine. "We were given this wine by my great-uncle Rick on our wedding night. It's a Châteauneuf-du-Pape. We've been saving it for a special occasion. Our retirement party, perhaps?"

"So why not today?" my dad cheered.

Serena sipped the wine, made a sour face, and hurled the glass across the room. It shattered our family portrait, which dripped with burgundy. My parents just stood there like scolded dogs.

I quickly checked the baby monitor. Theo was turning in his sleep, grimacing. He was going to sense Serena's presence and start crying any second now.

This witch is crazy. Grab Theo and go. Get her to follow you. Get her to chase you, like the night crawler chased you. Get her as far away from this house and Mom and Dad as possible.

Serena dabbed the wine from the corners of her mouth.

"Humans were born to serve us. This world needs to be set on fire from time to time, and I'm just the gal to light the match."

Serena held me in her lurid gaze. "The babysitters

163

have brainwashed you to think that we are the villains. But you'll see things differently once you've lived as one of us. Maybe I'll even enter you into our Annual Gala of Darkness, where I'm sure you'll win first prize."

She smoothed her Tom Ford–looking dress. "I have been alive long enough to learn one thing." She examined her exquisite rings and removed a diamond-encrusted beetle. "You can buy and sell anything in this world."

The bug-jewelry's sterling legs scuttled over plates, navigating around the salt and pepper. The sparkling insect looked up at me. It was stunning. And I don't like fancy stuff like that. The head of the beetle was an enormous, real-deal diamond. The biggest one I had ever seen. Not in real life. But on commercials for Zales.

There was suddenly a draw—an ancient power, greed, vanity—pulling at me.

"Keep it," Serena's voice said enticingly. "It's yours."

Candlelight flickered in the beetle's diamond head, rainbows shot from it, blurring my eyes. For a moment I felt dizzy and thought I heard a disco song echoing in my mind. I saw myself wearing the same white dress Serena was wearing. Victor was there too, and we danced and danced and danced.

"I have enchanted five-star generals into battle with the curl of my lips. I have toppled monarchies with the flick of my hair. And believe me, it's fun. Not a care in the world. I'm happy, Kelly. Light and free. And here you are, burdened with humanity. Give it up, sister. Choose beauty, and I can make you to die for."

It was the most gorgeous piece of jewelry I had ever seen, but I knew that if I put out my finger, I would be cursed to want jewelry and rich stuff more than life itself.

But still, if I sold this, I could give my family so many things. I could help my mom and dad pay their bills. Get my dad better health insurance. Get someone to help my mom out around the house, someone (besides me) to help her clean up, just for a little while. I could pay for those things and get us a new house.

"Now tell me, where is that beautiful, succulent baby?" Serena breathed heavily.

"With Dawn."

"And where is that? With Bullgarth? At that secret, silly cottage of yours? Tell me where the babysitters hide so I can rain fire upon them and sweep their ashes into the sea!"

"Isn't she lovely?" my father said.

Something pulled up my mother's smile, as if by invisible strings. "She sure is, Pete."

Serena shooed them away and leaned forward with an evil grin.

"Kelly, you are going to bring me that baby. Because as of right now, you are mine."

Something tickled my neck. A fist-sized spider had been crawling up my shoulder and was now leaning its hairy fangs down toward my jugular.

I grabbed a fork and jabbed it over my shoulder, pinning the spider to a wall.

"Nice try," I said. But it just came out as "AAAAH-HHHHH!!!"

I picked up my knife, slicing three more spiders that had lunged down from the ceiling.

"My babies!" Serena shrieked.

I flicked her diamond beetle ring across the table. She hissed and scrambled desperately for it.

A spider landed in the salad bowl. *Snap!* I slapped a plate over the salad bowl, trapping the spider inside.

"Catch her, my darlings!" Serena bellowed.

She stamped her foot, and her leather boots exploded into a fury of enormous spider legs. The bottom of her gown flared up, revealing an armored abdominal plate. Her eight black limbs smashed into the walls and the floor.

"Spuh-spuh-spuh . . . ," I mumbled in total shock.

"Spider!" Serena squealed with glee.

Clutching the salad bowl, I ran into the hallway.

"Kelly, don't be rude!" my mother said, charging after me.

"Little girl, come back here!" my father howled.

A horrible rumble shook the house. My parents' bedroom door burst open, and a wave of spiders spilled out, blanketing the hallway.

Spiders. Why did it have to be spiders?

The walls darkened with the hideous swarm. My feet were frozen. I was so overcome with fear I couldn't move.

Get off your tuffet and move it, Miss Muffet—that kid needs you!

I dove into my bedroom and slammed the door. *WHAM! WHAM!* The wave of beasties crashed against it.

In his little sleeper, Theo screamed.

I snatched a roll of duct tape and wound it around the salad bowl and plate to keep the spider trapped inside.

"Maybe Berna can use its venom to make an antidote to help your mommy and my mommy," I said to

Theo as I shoved it into my backpack.

Crack! Wood splintered behind me. Hundreds of spider legs scratched below the doorframe.

There was only one way out: the window above my desk. Luckily, my room was on the first floor. I buckled Theo into the Lone Wolf, flipped up the hidden panel on the stroller's handlebar, and pressed a button. The entire buggy went flat with all four wheels splayed out to the sides. I hoisted Theo and the compact L-Five outside.

The stroller came down hard on the grass, and then sprang up, locking back into position. Theo bounced in his seat. Stunned for a moment, he stopped crying.

I jumped out my window, rolling beside the Lone Wolf. Yanking on the handlebar, I snapped the hidden sword out of place—*SHINK!* The katana blade flashed in the moonlight.

"Surrender, Kelly," moaned my mother as she stumbled from the front door after me.

"Mom. Dad. I love you. But I gotta go."

My parents shrieked and chased after me.

"Hang on, T-Dog," I said, pressing the remote key.

The L-Five buzzed to life. I leaped onto the running boards and throttled the engine. With a high-pitched whine, the stroller took off more fast-and-furious than I expected.

The headlights of a black Rolls-Royce blinded me.

Two small, squashy trolls wearing weird medieval carnival masks were pointing out of the windshield. They were next to the ghost-faced chauffeur who was driving toward me.

I swung the stroller to the right and held tight, surfing the humming L-Five down a hill.

The street rushed under us. The Rolls-Royce rumbled inches behind me.

"Stop them!" screamed Serena as she scrambled from my house.

While I steered the L-Five, I chopped erratic swings, hitting the car's gleaming hood ornament. *CLANG! CLANG!*

"Back off! Baby on board!" I screamed.

The heavy roar of the engine gained. The driver's white, bloodless face was expressionless and cold, as if it was saying I was going to be roadkill.

Behind the car Serena's eight legs galloped after us. She sprang on top of the car's roof. Her thin legs clung to it as she shrieked at her chauffeur to run me over. She stabbed her enormous spider legs at me.

I sheathed the blade into the stroller's handle and pressed the button on the buggy marked OIL. The L-Five shot streams of slimy liquid onto the street.

The Rolls-Royce hit the shimmering puddle and spun out of control. The carnival-masked trolls growled and yelled as the pale driver fought with the steering wheel. Serena vaulted off the sideways-sliding car as it slammed into a tree with a shuddering blast.

"Don't text and drive!" I yelled.

I took a sharp turn up Old Doctor's Road. Theo was bobbing along in his seat like E.T. as the sidewalk raced beneath us. I leaned on the left running board, steering us under the weeping willow near my bus stop. Theo's blanket was fluttering around him, and he kept looking up at me like "What the heck is going on?"

I swerved the L-Five onto Hollyhock Avenue, hoping I was going to the right spot.

A stream of milky thread shot overhead like an arrow and splattered against a nearby telephone pole.

With growing panic I watched the spiderweb stretch.

WHOOSH! Serena's white gown rippled as she flew through the air, tethered to her soaring silk slingshot. She landed on top of a church steeple and balanced precariously on her talons.

I jammed my thumb down on **SMOKE**. Fog billowed in the air after us into massive black clouds that smelled like burning matches. I looked behind me, and Serena was on her perch, choking, the mist filling the street as she became a haze of dark limbs.

Serena's spider thread flew from the fog and snapped into another nearby telephone pole. She yanked back,

pulling the pole down. Power lines fell around me in a swarm of sparks and fire.

The Lone Wolf rocketed Theo and me through the sizzle and snapping wires.

The charge-battery light flashed on the handlebar.

"Not much juice left," I said. "Gotta make it count."

I veered the stroller toward a vast, snow-covered clearing, past a sign for Milton's Pond.

The wheels slushed across the frosted, icy pond.

"Please don't crack," I said.

Thwip! A tree shook as Serena swung down behind

us. She landed on the ice, her sharp claws skating across the surface.

An unsettling *crick-crack* raced under us.

The ice was breaking.

One of Serena's legs rose, about to skewer me, when she vanished with a splash into the icy water! Her limbs thrashed, churning the slushy pond.

Theo and I were almost to the shore. The stroller's back tires were sliding under the breaking ice that was collapsing right behind us.

The battery light blinked red.

"On Prancer, on Dancer, on Donner and Blizten!" I screamed, hoping for a Christmas miracle.

"Aaaadaaa!" screamed Theo.

We bumped onto the shoreline just as the ice collapsed into the pond and the engine died. We rolled to a stop. I looked back, breathless. In the middle of the pond, Serena struggled to hold her head above the water. Her fine braids had come undone and had fallen into wet strips. Her skin was bluish, and her eyes looked desperate as she doggy-paddled with her thin, trembling limbs.

"Come, child, help a poor damsel in distress, won't you?"

"Hm, let me think about that," I said, stroking my chin. "Nah."

She seemed genuinely helpless and hurt. Like a normal person in need.

I must have taken a step toward her, because she said, "That's it, help me, child. It's so very, very cold. You're very brave and good. That's right, child. Keep coming. That's a dear. Take my hand." Serena offered her hand to me.

I hesitated. "Give me the antidote to change back my parents and Dawn," I demanded.

"Of course. Whatever you want," she said.

"For real? No tricks?"

"Darling, in case you haven't noticed, I'm about to drown. What tricks could I possibly have?"

"Just because I'm a kid doesn't mean I'm an idiot!"

Serena's legs slashed out of the water.

"I'll never give you the antidote! I will exterminate you— My earrings!" she shrieked, and grabbed her ears. "Where are my earrings?"

She looked possessed, as if she could not live without her jewels.

"Later, alligator," I said.

"Adooooo," said Theo.

Serena scowled at me as I shot off, leaving her to become a spider-sicle.

"We will exterminate the lot of you!" she cried out with a gurgle. "Just like I took out your leader."

Wait, what? I choked. "Vee? What have you done with her?"

Serena gave me a final sneer. "The babysitters will fall. Just as she did."

I turned away so she couldn't see the tears in my eyes. I ran the L-Five up the snowy bluffs of Hangman's Hill and dialed Mama Vee's number. It went straight to voice mail.

I felt the trapped spider jostling around the inside of my backpack. I shivered at the sound of it clinking against the salad bowl.

If Mama Vee's gone too, we're in serious trouble.

The sparse lights of the suburbs sparkled below. I pushed the buggy down the hillside and rode the running boards as Theo and I skied the stroller over the snow.

A sinking loneliness swallowed me up. First Cassie and Curtis and now Vee? What would we do without Mama Vee?

I kept to the shadows, out of the streetlights. As I ran with Theo down the dark suburbs, not looking back, I flicked open my favorites on my phone and dialed Liz.

"Liz!" I shouted, excited to get someone on the phone who could help. "We just . . . ran–drove–away from Serena; she's here. I'm with Theo. She's in a pond. My parents– Oh my God, Liz– You have to come get us."

Over the phone I could hear *CRASH! SMASH! CLANG!*

"KEVIN, I TOLD YOU NOT TO TOUCH THAT!" Liz screamed. "I've got my hands full here, Ferguson. Might be a while before I can get to you. Down, Kevin! Don't punch that wall; you're going to—"

A loud crunch smashed over the phone. "Keeeeevin!" Liz whined.

I glanced back over my shoulder. Snow flurries curled between houses. "Vee's not picking up her phone, Liz," I said, pulling Theo's fuzzy blanket up to his red nose. He was twisting and turning in his seat. I gently put my hand on his chest. It felt warm and fragile. I had to get him out of the cold.

"AW, YOU'RE MAKING A MESS! Look, find shelter and hide. Not you; I was talking to Kelly! Don't hide in the closet, Kevin. Send me your location, and I'll get to you soon as I get Kevin to sleep. Hey, Kev, I'll play you some music— WUGNOT! YOU GOTTA PICK UP KELLY!"

The sound of the rec room's grand piano being banged on pierced my eardrums. "Kevin, don't play with that!" was the last thing I heard from Liz before she clicked off.

The heaviness of my soggy, frosty jacket and the aching cold of my blue fingers demanded I get help. I needed to get the little turtle somewhere safe and warm.

I knew one person who lived nearby: Tammy. And I knew the way there by heart. I'd been going there since I was five, after all. I pushed Theo up to the curb in front of Tammy's house and stood there. Candy canes lined the path to her door. I swallowed. Why was I so nervous, even though I had been here a thousand times?

Tammy swung open the door. "Is that a baby?" she said, pointing at Theo.

"Well, yeah. I'm babysitting. Can we come in?"

"Uh. Sure."

I looked over my shoulder, praying the Spider Queen was at the bottom of the pond. "I went for a walk with the baby, and this, um, person is following me. I just ran and . . ."

"Oh my gosh! Are you okay?" Tammy gasped, and pulled Theo and me inside, locking the door.

I choked. I couldn't bring myself to say anything. I was too shaken and cold and afraid, and I didn't want to involve her any more than I had to. I just wanted to get Theo warm and fed and have Wugnot come pick us up.

As I sent my location to Liz, wicked laughter squawked from Tammy's bedroom. I snapped to attention. Creatures were in her bedroom. I moved to protect Tammy.

"Sounds like a flock of witches," I whispered.

Tammy laughed. "It's Deanna and the Princess Pack."

They were huddled on Tammy's bed, all staring at their phones, giggling. Their eyes were like dull, blue diamonds in the screen's glow.

"Ladies and gentlemen, it's time for everyone's fabulous freak show, Kelly Ferguson!" Deanna said when she noticed me. Her head jerked back when she saw Theo. "I didn't know you had a baby."

"I'm babysitting, Deanna," I said.

"Fun for you!" she groaned.

"Is your mom here?" I asked Tammy.

"She'll be home in a little. They just came over to study," Tammy said.

"Gadoooo," Theo said.

I plugged the stroller into the wall, charging the battery.

"You should totally audition for *Teen Mom*," Deanna said into her screen.

The Pack laughed. Tammy frowned. "Someone was chasing Kelly," she said.

They looked up from their phones, wide-eyed. I wasn't intimidated by Deanna like I used to be, but I was not in the mood to lock horns with her, either. I had to focus on my mission: protect Theo.

"I'm gonna go wash up," I said, picking Theo up.

"You can leave him with us while you go to the bathroom," Deanna said, patting the empty space between them. "Babies love me. I'm going to adopt like a million of them one day from all over the world."

I checked her neck. No spider bite. But still . . . No way was I leaving Theo with them.

I darted into Tammy's kitchen pantry and grabbed the salt. In the bathroom, I dialed 9-1-1. As I poured salt down the sink, I told the operator my house had been broken into and I was not home, but my parents were there, and would they pretty please with sugar on top send a squad car or whatever to my house to check on my parents?

"Yes, we can do that, miss," said the 9-1-1 operator. "Are you in a safe place?"

"Yeah, but it's superawkward. See, my best friend decided to trade me in for a bunch of mean girls," I said. "So I'm physically safe but not, like, emotionally safe. Hello?"

"The police are on their way."

A floorboard creaked. Shadows glided under the bathroom door. I shoved it open and saw Deanna and the Princess Pack huddled outside.

"Oh, hi!" Deanna said. "We were just wondering if you wanted a little makeup?" She held up her bedazzled makeup bag. "I've been watching this Instagram model's YouTube tutorials on makeup. I'm supes good at it."

I looked at their dramatically dark eye shadow and cherry bomb–colored lips. "No thanks. I'm good."

"Oh, come on, Kelly Perfect Per-Ferguson! Have some fun-gerson," Deanna said, shoving her way into the bathroom with the others.

"Please stop talking like that," I said.

Tammy followed us in. I started to object, but their brushes and blushes and liners and glosses flew in my face, under Deanna's very specific instructions. I held my hand over Theo's head.

"You're getting glitter on his head!" I scolded.

The girls laughed. I felt strangely welcomed. Like I was part of their inner circle. They all looked so happy and carefree. I clung to Theo as Tammy tugged at my hair and combed it back. I hated to admit it, but it was kind of fun.

"Can I just say something?" Deanna whispered, dusting my eyelids with a brush. "Tamara told me what you told her about me being a total nasty-nass to you, and I know I can be a big ole meanie. But that was the old me. New me is mature and accepting of all kinds. I've gotten very socially conscious with my life. Just look at the stuff I post. It's like, we need to wake up to the world around us and see we're not like the most important thing all the time. The world is bigger than us, you guys. And so that's why I can say, and I know this is a total shocker, but I was wrong."

"So wrong," agreed the Princess Pack.

"But that me was, like, fake news," Deanna said. "I blame society and social media and so many other things for me being that way."

"I am so confused," I said.

"Voilà! This might be my masterpiece," Deanna said proudly.

CLICK! One of the princesses snapped a picture of me.

"You should send that to Victor," Deanna said, jabbing a makeup pencil under my eye. "He and I used to carpool together, you know. I had such a crush on him, but he's not my type anymore. But you should totally go for it."

The bathroom felt like it was getting smaller. Their brushes poked me, as if I were a rat in a lab experiment.

"Enough!" I shouted, elbowing away from them, holding Theo tight. "Get away!"

"What's your problem?" snapped Deanna.

Keeping my eyes on their stunned faces, I slowly backed out of the bathroom and stalked into Tammy's bedroom. I buckled Theo into the Lone Wolf. My hand hovered by one of the hidden swords as they followed me inside.

"What's wrong?" Tammy asked, sounding genuinely hurt.

"I'm not falling for this!" I screamed. "You're not

nice, Deanna! You've been mean to me and to Tammy our whole lives; that's how I know none of this is real! You've been bit– You've all been bit, and you can stop pretending because I'm on to you fakes! You liars!"

Deanna's face twisted in a grimace. She started to cry.

"This is the thanks I get for being nice." Deanna sobbed into her hands.

The Princess Pack gently comforted her. Tammy shook her head. Deanna's weeping sounded so real. So genuine.

That's because it is real, you idiot.

I blinked and caught my reflection in the mirror. Deanna had done a really good job on my makeup. I looked way older. At least fifteen. Maybe even sixteen.

"Sorry," I said, cringing. "It's been a really bad night for me."

Deanna blew her nose hard and straightened up. "It's okay. I get it. I intimidate people." She wiped her eyes and suddenly brightened. "Hey! I have an idea. Let's play Hail Harriet."

Hail Harriet was a creepy game kids in Rhode Island have been playing for decades. It was the local version of Bloody Mary. It was rumored that if you turned off the lights, lit a candle, and said "Harriet Hargrave" three times while looking into a mirror, you would see the ghost of Harriet Hargrave, the infamous mansion murderer, in the reflection. Given my present circumstances and the fact that Curtis and Cassie had disappeared while investigating Hargrave Manor, this game was the last thing in the world I wanted to play.

"No way," I said.

"Too late. You were mean, and now you have to do what we want," said Deanna, shutting off the lights. "I know how much you love weird stuff. I've heard rumors about you and the babysitters."

"Sounds spooky. I'm into it!" Tammy said, lighting a candle.

They gathered before the mirror and began to chant the gruesome rhyme:

> *"Harriet Hargrave, child, what did you do?*
> *Snipped and clipped your family in two.*
> *Did you mistake your parents for a hedge?*
> *What evil thing sent you over the edge?"*

"Seriously, you guys," I said. "I'm not playing."

But they kept going: "Harriet Hargrave, what else will you do? Say her name three times, and she'll come for YOU."

Shadows darkened. Theo stirred in my arms. He wasn't crying. *Yet.*

Their voices were low and eerie: "Harriet Hargrave. Harriet Hargrave."

The hair on my arms rose. "Cut it out!"

Deanna looked at me in the mirror and smirked. She was loving seeing me so freaked out.

"Harriet Hargrave."

We stood in the silent darkness, staring into the mirror. Deanna suddenly screamed. I jumped. The girls shrieked and grabbed one another.

"Got you!" Deanna cackled, pointing in my face. "You guys are such snowflakes!"

The other girls giggled and playfully shoved Deanna. I sighed and shook my head, but as they walked away from the mirror, I saw the candle flame flicker in an invisible wind.

"Is the heat on?" asked one of the Princesses. "I'm freezing."

Deanna, Tammy, and the Princesses went back to checking their phones. Theo started to cry. I anxiously looked around the room. We were alone. But why was Theo crying? He wasn't hungry or tired or stinky. Something dark caught my eye. In the mirror a teenager with black pigtails and a ragged floral-print dress was standing at the foot of the bed. Her head tilted at an odd angle. She was holding something behind her back.

Tammy's dresser thumped as I backed into it. Harriet's scowling eyes snapped in my direction.

"Take your meds, Kelly. It was just a joke," said Deanna.

Harriet's gaze locked on Theo. She smiled hungrily, and inky sludge ran down her pale chin, dripping down her dress.

"Go away," I whispered, snatching my backpack.

"Don't tell me to go away. We're in my room—you go away," Tammy said.

"Don't you see? She's right there!" I said, pointing frantically.

"Hardy har-har," Tammy said flatly as Harriet Hargrave stood beside her.

Wonderful. Now I could add being able to see ghosts to my list of weirdo abilities.

I swung Theo toward the door. *SLAM!* A roaring wind banged it shut. The girls yelped. I tried to open it, but it was being held closed by an invisible force. Tammy slapped on the lights. *Pop!* The bulb shattered. The door bucked and rattled. Harriet giggled, high-pitched, as if she were playing an amusing game.

"Stop it, Kelly," Tammy demanded.

Harriet walked through her. Tammy shuddered.

"Leave us alone!" I screamed, ripping the door open and running into the hall with Theo.

The teen spirit followed me from the bedroom and raised a pair of rusty hedge clippers from behind her back, slowly stepping toward me.

27

"The forces of darkness can kiss my butt, because you are not getting this baby!" I screamed, bolting into the living room, where I hid behind the blinking Christmas tree and opened the guide.

FROM Kelly FeRguson's copy
of A Babysitter's Guide to MonsteR Hunting:

GETTING RID OF A GHOST

Is the spiRit fRiendly? If so, hooRay! See
Aiding FRiendly Ghosts on page 32. FoR ghosts
summoned using boaRd games, tuRn to O foR
OUIJA.

If the ghost has been determined not to be friendly, SUCKS FOR YOU. Here are your options:

1) Show no fear. Ghosts don't listen to those they do not respect. Be brave.

2) Give the bones of the ghost a proper burial. (You will need bones and a rabbi/priest/pastor/imam with you to conduct the burial.)

3) Does the ghost have unfinished business? Help them finish it! Unless the unfinished business involves anything harmful/illegal/murderous/vengeful. (For vengeful reconciliation of spirits, see Healing and Peacemaking on page 45.)

4) Point the Amulet of Taka Ra at them and repeat the following: "Klatu veracta Nektu." Important note: for this method you will need the Amulet of Taka Ra. If you do not have the amulet, skip this step.

5) Electrical weaponry can be useful in dispersing a ghost and scattering its energy patterns into the ether. See P for Photon Pack.

6) Cast off your mortal coil, become a ghost yourself, take the spirit by the hand, and personally lead them into the light. (This is for emergencies only and must be done with

the assistance of a professional.) For more specifics, see F for Flatlining on page 245.

7) If all else fails, shout "YOU ARE NOT WELCOME" as you spin around in a circle three times while showing you are not afraid. Then say, "YOU HAVE NO POWER OVER ME." Warning: this might scare it away or this might make it angrier, and it will make you very dizzy.

My options seemed limited. None of the weapons in my backpack would work. I looked around for Harriet, but she wasn't there. Near the couch, a robotic Santa Claus waved its mechanical arm slowly back and forth. Ornaments on the tree branches shuddered. I saw in the shiny glass balls the warped reflection of Harriet Hargrave lunging at me. I dove out of the way, holding Theo like a football. The tree crashed into the wall. Ornaments shattered.

"She's gone insane!" Deanna said with a smirk. She, Tammy, and the rest of the Princess Pack were standing by the doorway.

Giggling, Harriet Hargrave grabbed Christmas knickknacks from the mantel and chucked them at the girls. Tammy got pelted with an Elf on the Shelf. Deanna took a Christmas stocking full of candy to the face.

Harriet picked up the tree by its trunk and swung it around the living room. The girls froze in shock. They couldn't see Harriet, but they could see the seven-foot-tall Christmas tree flailing in midair.

"Stop being so aggressive, Kelly!" shouted Deanna.

"Um. Kelly. How are you doing that?" Tammy said, quietly stunned.

"I'm not! It's Harriet Hargrave!"

The girls gawked at the hovering Christmas tree as it chased them down the hall. The girls shrieked and ran into Tammy's bedroom, locking the door. Harriet cackled and tossed the tree at me.

"Harriet Hargrave," I commanded. "By the Order of the Rhode Island Babysitters I order you to leave this house!"

Harriet snipped her hedge clippers at me, opened her mouth impossibly wide, and screeched out a foul wind.

So much for shouting her out of the house.

I stood my ground, clutching Theo against my hammering heart. *Snip, snip* went Harriet's clippers. The guide said to not show fear, but I was one scream away from peeing my pants. Ornaments that were scattered across the floor crunched under my sneakers as I backed into the living room. The robotic Santa waved and smiled. An overloaded wall socket stuffed with ten power strips crackled and sparked, causing the Christmas lights that jammed into it to pulse in the dark windows.

"Aaaaanaaaa," Theo grumbled into my sweater.

Snip, snip grated the creepy clipper blades as Harriet stalked toward me.

"You leave my friends alone!" I screamed at the apparition, glancing at the electrical socket. "Okay, so I'm not exactly besties with Deanna, but that doesn't mean I'm going to let you hurt her or the princesses! They're actually cool—just a little narcissistic, and I guess I'm jealous if I'm honest, but whatever, that's my own thing. If Tammy wants to hang out with other people, then fine! Just leave them alone and get out of this house!"

Harriet dove at me, clippers wide open for my throat. I ducked, and with my free hand, grabbed a string of Christmas lights off the window. I threw them at the hedge clippers just as the blades snapped closed, cutting into the wire.

Sparks shot through Harriet. She jolted and shrieked as the string of bulbs popped like fireworks. Smoke shot from her pigtails. I shielded Theo just before she burst into a thousand whizzing, screaming sparks.

Tammy's bedroom creaked open.

Tammy and the Princess Pack cautiously poked their heads around the corner and saw me standing in the wreckage.

"You. Wrecked. My. House," Tammy said quietly.

"It was the ghost of Harriet Hargrave," I said.

"Are you for real serious right now? You expect us to believe a ghost did this?" Deanna said.

I was speechless.

Deanna crossed her arms and glared at me. "You know, Kelly, we were trying really hard to be nice to you because we felt bad that you made up some story about being stalked, just so you could invite yourself over since you're so, like, heartbroken that Tamara is hanging out with us now. . . . But then you go and trash her house? I'm not the worst. You are. You're like the 'Grinch who stole Christmas' worst."

I looked to Tammy for a little support, but she avoided my eyes. My cheeks flushed.

The house I'd spent so much time in felt alien and unfamiliar with the angry faces of the Princess Pack and my now ex–best friend. Then an even worse realization dawned on me: the ghost of Harriet Hargrave was not gone for good. Can't kill something that's already dead, the guide says.

What if Harriet, once she rematerializes or whatever, tells Serena I'm here with Theo?

As frustrated as I was with Tammy and the Princess

Pack, the last thing I wanted was for them to be attacked.

My location had been compromised, and there was only one thing to do: keep moving. Stay ahead of the game.

"I should go," I said, buckling Theo into the Lone Wolf.

"I think you should," Tammy said.

"And you will be getting a bill for all the damage you've done here," Deanna called out.

Snow whirled inside as Tammy opened the front door. I bundled Theo up and zipped up my jacket in the doorway.

"I'm sorry," I said, looking out at the cold night. "Really. I didn't mean for any of this to happen."

Tammy chewed her lip and made sure we were out of earshot of Deanna and the others.

"I believe you," she whispered. "About Harriet. I don't know how, but I felt something wicked back there. And . . . I thought I saw something in the mirror. Someone. There was no way you could have made that tree do that. Is there?"

Her eyes met mine and saw I had told the truth. She gasped and put her shaking hand to her mouth.

"So actually, this is stupid Deanna's fault for wanting to play that game," she said, scowling into the house.

"Don't blame her," I said. "She's clueless. I gotta go,

Tammy. I'll explain everything soon, swearsville."

"Please don't go," she said, suddenly clutching my hand. "Stay. I'll tell them to leave."

My eyes welled up for a second. This was the real Tammy I knew. My bestie. It felt good to reconnect with her, if just for a second. It gave me a little bit of hope.

"Lock your doors. And watch out for spiders," I said, walking down the path.

"But you said it's not safe out there!" she pleaded.

"It's okay, Tammy. I'm a babysitter."

FROM BABYSITTER CASE FILE #13:
Professor Gonzalo

Among the Golden Age mansions lavishly decorated for Christmas, Hargrave Manor—with its crumbling rooftop and boarded-up windows—sat like the wicked stepchild of the neighborhood who refused to celebrate the season. Not a single flicker of light or good cheer escaped its dark, decaying roost.

With the help of her pale chauffer, the Spider Queen hobbled through the mansion. Her ten elegantly dressed, bleach-blond trolls, with their hair done up in curls and pompadours, paraded behind her, drying her with towels and covering her with fresh, long red robes. They wore colorful porcelain carnival masks painted with pretty smiles because their queen could not stand the sight of their hideous troll faces.

The queen flung open the door to her bedroom, where thick spiderwebs crisscrossed the chamber like banners of elegant lace. Clusters of gooey spider eggs hung from sinewy threads.

She looked into a mirror. Her makeup had been washed away, and her face was starting to look like a melted prune. Beneath her own skin, the face of something hideous waited to be exposed.

"Disaster!" she hissed, shattering the mirror.

In their translucent sacs, baby spiders twitched at the sound of their mother's voice.

"She is only a child! A thirteen-year-old ginger! A worm!"

Her chauffer held out his wrists, and she set upon them,

drinking in a frenzy, draining his body to the brink of death. Having a corpse for a driver was as good as having no driver, so she let him live.

"Professor Gonzalo! Get in here now!"

A tubby, pear-shaped man wearing a tweed jacket and a bow tie cautiously poked his head into her room. Professor Gonzalo's tiny, cruel eyes blinked behind his dirty spectacles. Though he was the fifth Boogeyman, he feared Serena.

"Yes, my queen?" said the eager Professor.

"I need to feed," she said.

"I'll bring something up from the cellar immediately." The Professor's sweaty upper lip curled into a smile. "We caught another visitor while you were out. A babysitter."

Serena's fangs lowered. She threw back her hair and her jewels sparkled like stars on a summer night. "Aaaaaaah."

She noticed the Professor staring at her wrinkled face; her sagging mouth and lopsided eye. The horrified look in the Professor's eyes in reaction to her sudden ugliness embarrassed her. Kelly the babysitter had done this to her. And Kelly the babysitter would suffer for all eternity for it.

"What are you waiting for? Fetch me my dinner!" she shouted.

The Professor scrambled away, bowing.

"Makeup!" snapped Serena.

Her makeup artist—troll nervously dragged over a treasure chest filled with enchanted beauty products, procured from witch doctors and voodoo priestesses from around the world.

A spider dipped its legs inside a jar of concealer and expertly tapped cover-up under the queen's eyes. As spiders scurried across her face, applying lipstick and rouge, the queen watched her skin magically lighten and glow to perfection. She blew a kiss at her reflection.

"That's more like it. Mama looks gooooood."

The spiders kissed her on the cheek and applauded.

Dust disturbed by a strange breeze curled around them. Static electricity crackled as shadows swirled into the shape of a sixteen-year-old girl with black pigtails and a sour, scornful expression.

"Ah, Miss Hargrave," said Serena. "How nice to finally see you. Thank you for letting my servants and me stay in your lovely home. I hope we haven't disturbed you or your family?"

With croaking tones, Harriet Hargrave told the monster queen of the terrible thing the young babysitter had done to her, and then she told them where they could find her.

Pushing the baby buggy through the icy suburbs, I saw the lonely blue glow of a television in the window of a house that was not decorated for Christmas. An elderly man was watching TV. I thought of banging on his front door and asking for help, but then I saw through his hazy curtain that he had an oxygen tank by his chair. He wheezed and breathed into a foggy rubber mask as the Rockettes danced across the screen.

Icy wind buzzed, rattling Christmas lights against houses. It sounded like chattering teeth.

"Eeeeh, eeeeh," said Theo.

"Okay, Big T.," I whispered. "What's the plan?"

"Daddoooo daddddsseeee."

"Okay."

"DaadOOOO daddSEEEE!"

"That's exactly what I was thinking. We keep a low profile until Wugnot picks us up. Head back to HQ. Give Mr. Eight Tap Shoes in my backpack to Berna, see if she can make an antidote for Serena's poison out of it."

Theo's eyes sparkled. I took a deep breath.

"And then, we get rid of Serena and her spiders."

And then what? We would inject the antidote into each of the infected, one by one?

I shuddered at the tasks ahead. It all seemed so impossible.

"I don't know, Big T." I sighed. "I'm just me. And you, no offense, you're a baby. Not exactly the deadly duo. Let's get you someplace safe till Wugnot finds us. I don't feel like playing hide-and-seek in subzero temps with Serena's minions."

A warm light rose in the distance. I pushed the stroller toward the peak of a red-and-white-striped big top tent. The bright smell of fresh evergreens greeted me. A banner hung over the entrance: "Old Nick's Tree Patch."

Yes! I love Christmas tree lots. This is the perfect place to wait.

I walked under the tent, past a life-sized, wooden Nativity scene. There were so many Christmas lights that they cast a soft halo around us. Not exactly a secret hideout, but it would have to do.

As families shopped around us, I dialed Berna's number and gave her the full scoop.

"You have a spider in your bag?" Berna said.

"Yeah. Don't remind me. I die a little every time I feel it move. How close is Wuggie?"

"He's gonna be a little late."

"What part of 'I'm being hunted' don't you guys get?"

"We are doing the best we can with what we've got right now. We're down three sitters, and now Liz and Kevin have gone AWOL."

"What happened?"

"Liz was playing music to Kevin," Berna continued. "That kid can dance to some Gaga. He was stomping around. I thought he was going to break through the floor. Then he saw a picture of Liz and him when they were kids . . . His family, y'know. And Kevin threw a big ole tantrum."

GRRRRZZZT! The earsplitting sound of a buzz saw made me jump. The Christmas tree–seller guy had a tree laid on a saw machine and was chopping the end off the stump. The grating sound gave me the chills.

"He wanted to see his parents. Liz explained that they were divorced and that things hadn't been so good the past few years since Kevin went missing. Well, Kevin started crying, and he ran out the door to go and find them."

"He's out?" I yelped.

"Wugnot tried to stop him, but Kevin knocked him out of the way. Went full beast mode on Wugnot."

"Kelly?" said a voice behind me.

I froze. I knew that voice. It was the voice of rainbows and chocolate. I turned around. There he stood, beside the Christmas trees, wearing his backpack, a puffy blue jacket, and a beanie over his shaggy black hair, which fell over his eyes. Victor.

"I'll call you back, Bern," I mumbled into the phone.

"What are you doing here?" he asked.

"Y'know. Babysitting! Duh!" I tried to laugh, but it came out weird. No surprise. "What brings you here?"

"Getting a tree," he said, pointing to his family.

His burly dad and cute mom were inspecting a North Valley Spruce, grumbling about the price. His little brother and sister swatted each other with broken branches.

"Well, hiiii, everybody! I mean, *hola, amigos*; *familia de* Victor! This is not my baby. *No es mi bambino.* I'm a babysitter. Not a mommy."

Stop sounding so dorky. Just talk normal. I can't! This is his family!

Victor's mom smiled at me. *"¿Quién es?"*

Victor's dad elbowed his mother and whispered: *"Es ella."*

204

Victor's mother nodded. "*Sí*, yes. Hello, Kelly."

They know about me?

I vigorously shook their hands. Victor's mother caught sight of Theo, and she became transfixed, drawn toward the stroller. A huge grin broke out on her face. She beckoned Victor's father over. The whole family admired Baby Theo.

"*Angelito*," Victor's father said.

He made the sign of the cross, kissed his fingers, and then reached out and placed them on Theo's forehead. I leaned over and checked the backs of all their necks.

No spider bites. All clear.

"Are you wearing makeup?" Victor said in half question, half wonderment.

I felt my cheeks flush. "Uh. Yeah. No biggie," I scoffed, trying to sound cool. "Makes me feel more professional when I babysit."

What are you saying?

Victor spoke Spanish to his parents, and they cast suspicious glances at me. From what I understood of their argument, Victor asked if he could stay to walk me home. Or he really wanted to buy some cheese at the beach. My Spanish is not that good.

Finally, his parents agreed.

"Nice to meet you, Kelly. Victor, we will see you at home in ten minutes. *Diez*."

I waved good-bye as they dragged their tree off,

leaving Victor and me and Theo alone amid the small forest, under the twinkling lights.

This is our Fault in Our Stars *moment!*

"You're shaking," said Victor.

"It's cold."

Nothing to do with your big brown eyes staring into my soul.

"Let's walk to my house and wait there."

I shook my head. "I'll be okay. Wugnot's picking me up. You can go."

The light in his beaming eyes dimmed. "You don't think I can handle being a babysitter, do you? You saw my little brother and sister. I grew up changing their stinky diapers."

"That's not it."

"Am I not good enough to be in your club?"

"First, it's an order, not a club. And second, you're more than good enough. Is that why you were so upset with me at school?"

"I guess."

"Well, I didn't mean to make you feel that way. If I'm honest, I'm the one who doesn't feel worthy. There's all this pressure on me to be awesome, and I'm not really living up to it at the moment. I would never want to make you feel the same."

"Well, you kind of are. And what are you talking about? You're great."

"You're catching me between failures," I said. "I never meant to make you feel not good enough. It's just . . . There's this rule. Law, actually."

"What law?"

I cringed. "Can't we just, like, drink some hot chocolate and talk about other things? It's been a doozy of a night."

"What law, Kelly?"

I sighed and opened the *Babysitter's Guide to Monster Hunting* and showed him

Law Number Three: no crushes allowed while sitting.

Victor looked confused. Then his dimple appeared. He glanced at me.

"Does this mean I'm . . . your . . . ?"

"High five!"

He gave me a weird look and high-fived me. Not the most romantic gesture, the high five, but I didn't know what else to do.

"This is very strange," he said.

"Strange? I pour my heart out, and all you can say is that's strange?" I snapped the guide shut. "Let's go, Theo."

I pushed the stroller away, but then I felt Victor's warm hand hold on to my arm. He pulled me close.

I could smell the Dr Pepper Cherry on his breath.

I could feel his heart thumping in his chest.

"Victor, if we're together," I said slowly, "bad things will happen."

"This doesn't feel bad to me."

You're right. This feels like giggles and puppies.

I swear, mistletoe was hanging right above our head.

"When I am with you," he whispered, low and soft, "only good things happen."

This is the part where he kisses you. What do I do? I NEED CHAPSTICK! DOES ANYONE HAVE ANY CHAPSTICK? MEDIC!

His face filled my eyes. I puckered my lips and—

Click.

The string of lights shut down around us. The Christmas music under the tent stopped. We were plunged into darkness.

"Lot's closed!" called the gruff tree-seller guy. "Time to go, kids."

A cold wind raced through the branches.

"Eeeeea!" cried Theo.

The romantic flutter in my belly was replaced with a creepy feeling.

"Uh-oh," I said, tensing. "Theo's monster radar. Something's coming."

I scanned the darkness. Along the street, I saw the Rolls-Royce driving slowly through the neighborhood like a shark patrolling the ocean. The pale chauffer and the eerie masked trolls were peering from the windows, scrutinizing the area.

I gasped, grabbing Victor and Theo, and we ducked

behind a patch of noble firs. One of the masked trolls pointed in my direction, and the creepy car drove toward us.

The Rolls-Royce rumbled to a stop in front of the Christmas tree lot. Icy mist plumed from its exhaust. Headlights cast long black shadows through the trees. It was as if the babysitter universe wanted to punish me for having a crush.

"Sorry, folks. Lot's closed," the Christmas tree seller said to the driver.

From our hiding place Victor and I watched the car window roll down.

The seller leaned toward the driver. "You hear me in there?"

A flash of black fur pounced in the man's face. He stumbled back as the spider clamped itself on his mouth. I closed my eyes in terror. Victor's breath quickened.

"*Dios mío.*"

"Quiet!" I whispered, looking for the best exit route.

Three masked trolls hopped from the Rolls-Royce. Their snotty noses snuffled as they entered the tent. Behind them, the tree seller rose to his feet with a possessed look in his eyes.

"There's two kids in there," said the bitten seller. "One of them's got a baby."

Thanks a lot, mister.

I pushed the stroller through the labyrinth of Christmas trees. Victor followed close behind me and picked up a long branch.

"I'll protect you, Kelly." He swung it around like a staff. "I've been practicing my babysitter-fu."

"Now is not the time for heroics," I said.

"Now is the perfect time for heroics!" he said.

The pitter-pat of little spidey feet rolled across the ground. Spiders swished through the trees, searching for us.

Victor squealed. I clamped my hand over his mouth, muffling his scream.

GRRRZZZZT! A troll had turned on the buzz saw machine. The little creep clapped with glee as the blade spun. Our game of hide-and-seek was about to end with us drowning in bugs and then being chopped to pieces.

This really is our Fault in Our Stars *moment. One of us is going to end up dead!*

I pushed Theo toward the back of the tent. Victor swept away a few arachnerds away from our feet, but the eight-legged flash mob scurried around us.

Climbing, leaping, clicking.

Their jeweled eyes sparkled as the spiders bobbed back and forth on their spiky fingerlike legs.

I saw their little pincers and fangs, and my body did

an impression of wet spaghetti.

I reached in my book bag and threw handfuls of jelly beans onto the floor in front of me. The crawlies gobbled them up and marched at me.

"You're feeding them?" Victor said. "Are you crazy?"

"Do you not think I know what I'm doing?"

In seconds we'd be buried in a mass of legs and pincers, but I had to get this off my chest.

"Answer the question. Do you or do you not think I know what I'm doing?"

"Yeah! I dunno. This is kind of a lot to take in."

"I'll take that as a yes," I said, pouring jelly beans in his hand.

He tossed them at the spiders, and they gobbled them up.

One of the spiders in front of me began to shake and jitter like the lid on a boiling pot. Squeal! *Boosh!* In a burst of purple sludge, one exploded, leaving nothing but its legs. Squeal! *Boosh!* Another one popped. Squeal! *Kaboosh!* In rapid-fire succession an entire row of enormous bellies detonated like firecrackers, painting the trees in purple muck.

"What kind of jelly beans are these?" said Victor, inspecting one.

"The exploding kind," I said. "Don't eat them."

The other spiders shrieked, clambering over one another other to dive back into the Rolls-Royce.

I saw one of the trolls lift his mask, and his pug nose sniffed the air. The rest bounded through the trees, their gooey nostrils flared.

They can smell us. . . .

I caught a whiff of Theo's diaper. Ripe and pungent.

"They can smell Theo's diaper!"

"So can I," Victor whispered. "His shorts are fully loaded."

That's how they know where we are.

"I have an idea," I whispered.

The trolls hopped to the back of the tent. They parted a stack of evergreens, and with leering smiles, found Theo's dirty diaper hanging from a branch.

Psych!

Meanwhile, Theo, Victor, and I were a block away, running and watching the trolls angrily look around for us. My dirty diaper decoy had bought us a little time, even if poor Theo had to go commando until we were safely out of range.

"High five!" I said, holding up my hand.

"Do you always high-five this much?"

"Nervous habit. Just slap my hand, please. I can't lower it until you do. It's a thing."

We slapped hands. I checked my phone. Wugnot had texted, saying he was right around the corner. As we ducked through backyards, I felt something stuck on my head. A severed spider leg was tangled in my hair.

We made our way to the corner of Oakdell and Pippin, where Wugnot was waiting in the babysitter mobile, rocking out to a death metal version of "Jingle Bell Rock."

"Who the fluffernutter this?" Wugnot said, jabbing his tail at Victor.

I loaded Theo into the back of the van. "Victor, Wugnot. Wugnot, Victor."

Victor made a shocked sound and stared at Wugnot.

I nudged Victor. "Hobgoblins don't like to be stared at."

Victor quickly looked away as Wugnot clicked his teeth.

"Any word from Vee or Cassie?"

"Was just going to ask you the same thing," said Wugnot, driving off.

"We need to go back to headquarters, get Berna to make an antidote; then we'll figure out a plan of attack on Hargrave Manor."

"Righteous." Wugnot suddenly snapped his fingers. "Oh, *that* Victor!"

I sank in my seat. "Please don't embarrass me, Wuggie."

"Don't you know Law Number Three?" announced Wugnot.

I growled at him.

Wugnot shifted gears, grinding the van's transmission.

"Which way to your house, Victor?" I asked.

"You're not getting rid of me that easy," Victor said.

"Oh yes I am," Wugnot said, slamming hard on the brakes. "Get one thing straight, boyo." Wugnot pointed his thumb to his chest. "I am a rules-based individual. Do you have any idea how much trouble I'd be in if I didn't follow the guide? And if it says no crushes on a job, then you can take a hike."

"Wugnot, be cool!" I said, my eyes bulging at how freely he said "crush."

But Wugnot was right. As much as I wanted Victor with us, it was too dangerous to continue to break Law Number Three.

Wugnot hopped out of the van and swung open the door. "Out!"

Victor crossed his arms and stayed put. Wugnot easily scooped Victor up and tossed him onto the sidewalk.

"Hit the bricks, kid," Wugnot growled.

"We can't just leave him here," I said.

"It's okay," Victor said, defeated. "I live down the block. I can walk. I don't want to cause trouble."

"But–" I started to say.

"Nice meeting ya," said Wugnot, yanking the van door closed and hopping back into the driver's seat.

I put my hand on the glass.

Forbidden love, thy name is Victor!

As Wugnot drove away, I looked in the rearview to watch Victor recede into the distance, like we were in some epic romantic movie, but he was already gone.

"I don't make the rules, Kelly. I just follow 'em," Wugnot said, slamming the gas.

"Don't talk to me," I said, staring out the window. "I'm pouting."

FROM LIZ'S JOURNAL

"Kev! Stop!"

I chased my was-little-but-now-giant monster brother past the frozen cranberry bogs to our old house. I hadn't been home since Mom left.

Kevin charged toward the window of our living room. Our dad was on the couch, watching the MMA Christmas Cage Match Royale.

I hopped off my dirt bike and tried to pull Kevin from the window, but the stinker growled, shaking my hand off his shoulder.

"What the devil?" I heard my dad gasp.

He sprang from the couch and wiped his mouth. "Thing from the news."

"Aaaaaooooooaaaadddd," moaned Kevin.

My dad ran from the living room. I had a terrible feeling I knew where he was going.

Dad returned, shotgun in hand.

"Run, Kevin!" I cried.

Kevin didn't budge. He stood there, panting.

"Lizzie?" my dad said, looking between the two of us, confused. "What are you doing with that thing?"

I took a deep breath and stood beside my hairy, beastly brother.

"Dad, this is Kevin."

Kevin's feet turned in. His giant paw innocently waved hello.

"Merrrrrmoooo," mumbled Kevin.

There was a small glimmer of recognition in my dad's eyes. Maybe it was because Kev always stood that way when he waved hello, with that same sweet, small look in his eye.

"That ugly freak of nature is not my son," said Dad.

Kevin threw back his head. "OOOOOOROOO!"

"Get out of here!" my father screamed, charging out of the house.

Distant dog barking erupted. The night filled with howls as Kevin ran away. My dad aimed his shotgun. My hand shot out, grabbing the barrel just as it boomed into the sky.

"Kevin, wait!" I called out, jumping onto my dirt bike.

I popped a wheelie and chased after him, leaving our dad in the dust.

Drivers on the highway screamed.

They swerved to avoid the eight-foot-tall furry creature on two legs. My bro scraped at the edges of a steel manhole cover.

"Don't go down there, you big oaf!" I shouted.

A truck horn blared. It was driving right toward him. Kevin flung the metal disk, barely missing the windshield as the truck thundered right over the open sewer.

Brakes squealed, and the rig shuddered to a stop. Kevin was gone.

I darted over the concrete divider and peered into the dark hole.

The echoes of Kevin's wails wafted up with the sludgy stink.

I flicked on my flashlight and dropped into the sewers.

Splash!

I tied a bandanna around my nose to block out the toxic smell, but that didn't help much. The reverberations of Kevin's sobs bounced off the moss-dripping patchwork. I found Kevin sitting at the edge of a small waterfall of sludge. He was staring into the well of water churning below, watching his angry tears be collected and washed down the drain.

I sat down beside him. Moonlight beamed through a sewer grate high above us.

"Dad didn't mean it, Kev."

Kev gloomily shook his head.

"One day he'll understand." I patted the sweaty clumps of fur on his back. "For now, we have each other. And I promise, I'm never gonna lose you again."

Kev wailed, pointed to himself and then to me.

"I love you too, little bro."

Kev threw back his head and howled at the moon. In harmony, I barked with him. "Arrroooooooh!"

WHAT LIZ DID NOT KNOW
(But Should Have Known)

Far across the sewers, Peskov the Sleeknatch was inspecting clumps of spider eggs that Serena's trolls had planted beneath the town, basking in the thick steam rolling off the river of sludge, when he heard the echoes of monster sobs and cries bouncing off the aqueduct walls.

The six-eyed meatball instantly recognized the cry of the queen's favorite servant. It was a sound it had heard many times.

The Sleeknatch rolled toward the noise, tumbling through the flies and gnat clouds. It slid down a moist concrete ramp, splashing into the muck. Its six eyestalks paddled through the slop with surprising speed. Excitement and desperation fueled it. The queen would be so pleased with it for finding Bullgarth.

The Sleeknatch stopped at the edge of a well. Looking up, its six wide eyes saw the hairy mutant talking with the girl with pink-and-black hair.

Liz. His human sister.

Imagine the Sleeknatch's surprise!

In its hiding place, the squashy Sleeknatch jiggled with glee. *Wait until the queen finds out about this.* Its reward would be handsome. It would become her favorite, and this hairy beast would be chained up for life.

The Sleeknatch followed the brother and sister as they walked out of the sewers. The sticky glob rolled itself after them, narrowly being missed by a racing car. The powerful, hairy giant and his sister were too fast for the roly-poly six-eyed ball of snot. But then it heard their cries in the distance, and the Sleeknatch was back on their trail.

Brambles and thorns stuck to the Sleeknatch's slimy skin as it somersaulted through swamps and bogs and backyards in pursuit of the babysitter and the traitor.

When he saw the babysitter open a secret pathway through the bushes and then lead her brother toward a brick cottage, the meatball creature let out a gurgling gasp. The large house looked like something out of a fairy tale. The Sleeknatch slithered its way after them, just as the hidden entrance closed behind it.

It watched the girl lean her dirt bike against a stone

lion and unlock the heavily fortified front door.

One of its bloodshot eagle eyes managed to glimpse por-
traits of babysitters hanging on the wall before the girl
led Bullgarth inside and shut the door.

The Sleeknatch's onion eyes bulged. It had found the
babysitters' secret headquarters.

The queen would surely reward it for this.

30

On the way to headquarters, we drove past my block. Blue and red lights illuminated the street. Neighbors in their pajamas clustered around two patrol cars parked by my house. No sign of my parents. Wugnot slowed down. The police crowded around us.

Officer Muntz and lanky Sheriff Heep stepped forward. Wugnot pulled his trucker hat over his eyes and slipped on a pair of thick, horn-rimmed glasses.

"Hello, officers. That's my house. Are my parents okay?"

"They're doing just fine, miss," said Muntz with a big smile.

The night seemed still. I glanced around the street.

Where did all the spiders go? And where were my parents?

Wugnot grunted, chewing on a toothpick.

"Ambulance took 'em," said Sheriff Heep with an even bigger smile. "Why don't you step out of the car, and we'll take you to them."

His heavy utility belt creaked. He had his nightstick in his hand. Even though it was freezing outside, his jaw was slicked with sweat.

My blood rushed in my veins.

"Actually, I think we're good," I said.

"Don't gotta tell me twice," Wugnot said, shifting into drive.

"WAAAAAAH!" cried Theo.

In unison, all the police and my neighbors turned their heads in our direction.

"She has the child," one of them whispered.

"Drive!" I screamed.

Wugnot's clawed foot slammed the gas.

Sheriff Heep grabbed at the van's door handle, and I saw two fresh spider pricks on his wrist before we sped away from his reach.

Neighbors charged toward us with evil in their eyes. "Give us the child!"

Sweet old Mrs. McGillicuty snarled at us. She had the nicest rosebushes on the block, and now she wanted to kill me.

"They're bit!" I screamed again. "They're all bit!"

"Move it or lose it, folks," Wugnot said calmly, looking over his shoulder.

The van flew backward, swerving across the street.

"Ahh!" I heard a cry from the back.

"Someone jumped on the van?" I said, looking out of the window.

Two legs swung out from behind the rear, flailing from side to side.

I'd recognize those sneakers anywhere.

"Victor?" I shrieked.

"Slow down!" Victor shouted, hanging on to the back of the van.

"Slow down!" I yelled at Wugnot.

Wugnot sped up.

Victor's head poked out from around the back. He was clutching the small ladder on the back door.

"Wugnot, why didn't you see him?"

"Windows are tinted so we don't get any lookie-loos." He shrugged. "That is very dangerous and stupid, pal! I'm telling your parents."

"Hang on!" I clambered into the back.

Wugnot jerked to a stop as I flung open the door and Victor climbed inside.

"I jumped on when you drove off," Victor said innocently.

"You idiot!" I said, shoving him away from my

face. "You could've been hurt! What are you trying to prove?"

The police patrol car raced after us, sirens wailing.

"Quit smooching and close the doors," Wugnot said.

His tail switched on the stereo, blasting heavy metal "Jingle Bells." "Gonna need to do a little off-roading," the wild hobgoblin said, glancing in the rearview. "Hang on to something."

The van slammed across the marshes.

"Is a silver bullet really the only way to kill a werewolf?" Victor asked Wugnot. "I've always wondered."

Wugnot growled and maneuvered us through the woods. "Little busy here, kid."

"Have you met the Loch Ness monster? Is it real? I know it is."

Branches scratched the metal doors, sounding like fingernails going down a chalkboard.

"Why you wanna be a babysitter, kid? You think it's cool? 'Cause I got news for you. The cool-wow-neat factor wears off pretty quick."

Victor thought about it for a moment. Then with a

serious look he said, "Let's just say, I don't like bullies."

I looked at Victor. He grew self-conscious.

"Fascinating story. Now put a sock in it, bub," Wugnot grunted, tossing a bandanna into my hands.

"Sorry," I said as I blindfolded Victor. "Protocol."

Wugnot pulled a lever, and a high-pitched air horn played a tune. The gnarled trees and vines parted before us. Through the secret entrance, up the gravel drive, past the stables. I took the blindfold off Victor's eyes.

"Whoa," he said.

"You're gonna start saying that a lot," I said, grabbing a sleeping Theo into my arms and leading him into our headquarters. "Just don't touch anything."

"Whoa!" he said, walking past the training room and into the laboratory where Dawn was asleep on a gurney.

Berna was FaceTiming with her mother. "I checked all her vitals, Mom. Kelly! Wugs! Victor?" Berna's eyebrow arched. "Well, hello, handsome."

"Hi, Mrs. Vincent!" I waved at her mom on Face-Time.

"I heard you didn't pass Heck Weekend," Berna's mom said.

"Great talking to you, too."

Berna shot me an amused smile. "I see someone didn't read Law Number Three."

228

I elbowed Berna. Dawn's heart rate monitor beeped. The bite on her neck was inflamed with sickly black-and-blue veins. Baby Theo sputtered awake.

A golden light shot down the chimney. In a burst of snowflakes, Penelope, the recon pixie, circled us in a flurry of chimes.

"Vee's in danger!" Berna said.

"You speak Pixie?" I asked.

"Her and Cassie and Curtis are at . . ." Berna narrowed her eyes and studied Penelope.

"Hargrave Manor," I said.

Cold fear twisted through me. Berna's eyes went big with worry.

"Muummmaaaa?" Baby Theo said, reaching out for Dawn.

"She's resting, little turtle. Berna's going to make her better," I said quietly.

I took the duct-taped salad bowl out of my backpack. "You said you might be able to make some kind of cure from the venom, right?" I asked. A rustling of lettuce skittered as the spider hissed inside.

I handed Theo to Victor and carefully peeled back the tape from the salad bowl.

"Grit of the Sandman, please," I asked Berna.

Berna rummaged through a rack of potions and handed me a bottle with glowing green liquid. I squeezed a few drops into the bowl and explained to

229

Victor that Grit of the Sandman was a monster potion that would knock most anything unconscious.

I carefully scooped out the spider from the wilted lettuce. My stomach gurgled into my throat. My swallow felt shallow. My head lulled forward. Everything got all woozy.

"You okay, Kells?" Berna said.

"I don't like spuh-spuh–" I gagged before I could finish my sentence.

"You got arachnophobia?" said Berna, shaking her head. "Go eat some chips or something."

"No," I said, standing firm. Also I didn't want to wimp out in front of Victor. "I gotta . . . get over this."

Its leg twitched as I set it down, belly up, on a metal tray. I jumped back, furiously shaking my hands. Berna's scalpel sliced open the spider's abdomen with an unsettling *squish*.

"Deees-gusting," Victor said, leaning closer.

"Gaah," I said, swallowing a ball of hot nervous stomach juices that was burning my throat.

"Venom glands are usually located in the chelicerae or under the carapace." Berna chomped on her gum as she poked around its slimy organs. "The ducts extend through the chelicerae and open near the tips of the fangs."

"Fascinating," said Victor with a giddy glint in his eye.

Berna snipped and sliced and then tweezed out a thick, juicy, purple venom sack dripping with slime. She blew a huge bubble that popped. "And there you have the venom gland."

She dropped it into a petri dish and stuck a syringe into it.

"Don't get any on you, and be very careful not to spill any," said Berna. "We need to inject the toxin in very small, controlled doses into some kind of animal. Then we extract the resulting antibodies from the host animal's blood and transfuse them into the patient." Berna held the needle up to the light.

She spun toward me. Berna looked like a mad scientist. "Wanna volunteer?"

"Can't you just try it out on Dawn?" I begged.

"I need clean blood to make the antidote. Dawn's already infected."

"Gimme a second. I gotta change Theo's diaper," I said, ducking out of the doorway.

I cleaned up Theo and laid him in a crib inside the nursery, locked the door from the outside, and then pulled a heavy cabinet in front of it when I heard Liz and Kevin down the hall.

They were in the library. Following Kevin's hand signals and grunts, Liz was drawing an outline of Hargrave Manor. Kevin shot to his feet, towering over me.

"Whoa, big fella," I said, putting up my hands and blocking the library entrance. "Is he cool?"

"Cooler than you," Liz smirked.

She pressed Play on her phone and pumped a pop-punk song, and Kevin's eyes lit up.

"Music chills him out," Liz said.

Bigfoot Boy's giant feet stomped the ground. *WHAM! WHAM!*

"I'll put that in the guide," I said, stepping back so my toes didn't get crushed.

Liz nodded to the Hargrave Manor drawing on the chalkboard. "Kevin knows a way that we can sneak inside," Liz said.

"Wonderful. Come to the lab. Berna needs a volunteer."

As I led Liz and Kevin down the hall, I tore a blank

page out of my notebook and ripped it into little strips and folded them up. In the lab I held the pieces of paper to Berna, Victor, Liz, Kevin, and Wugnot. Liz spotted Victor, and her eyes narrowed.

"Check the guide, newb," Liz said. "Law Number Three clearly states—"

I threw up my hands. "I know what it states! Everyone knows what it states! He's been very helpful! Now could we please stop talking about it?"

"Thank you," said Victor.

"Whoever draws the shortest strip has to be Berna's guinea pig," I said, quick to change the subject as I held up the papers.

Berna tapped the syringe. Kevin recoiled and ducked behind his sister.

Nice to know even eight-foot-tall beasts are afraid of needles.

Wugnot put up his hands. "Don't look at me. Monsters got different blood. Who knows what happens if that stuff gets into my veins." He left the lab in search of a snack.

"Swearsville one of us won't get turned into Serena's puppet?" I asked.

Berna shook her head tensely. "You won't. But I can promise you'll experience some nausea and flu-like symptoms."

"Vomiting and sickness? Sign me up," Liz joked,

233

taking a strip of paper.

We unfolded them and glanced at one another . . .
Victor chewed his lip.

"My lucky day," he said.

Berna held up the needle. Victor tensed. I reached
down and laced my fingers with his. He closed his eyes
and nodded.

REEEEEEP! REEEEEP!

A shrill siren whooped.

REEEEEEP! REEEEEP!

Emergency lights flashed, casting shadows across
the portrait of Serena that was leaning against the
couch, watching us with a victorious smile.

REEEEEEP! REEEEEP!

Down the hall, Wugnot screamed, "Stations! Something tripped the alarm!"

Wugnot darted into a wooden booth beside the training room and checked the small black-and-white security monitors showing the house perimeter. The front entrance was closed. The side garden was empty. The monster stables were secure.

"Nothing out there," Wugnot grunted, turning off the shrieking alarm.

The angular head of a giant locust looked down into security camera D. Wugnot recoiled, disgusted. A terrible buzz arose in the sky.

"Listen!" said Victor.

Skreeer-reeer-reeeee!

Foot-long locusts soared through the fog, icy mist trailing from their wings.

WHAM! A three-foot-long cockroach leg shattered the living room window. Human-sized cockroaches rose from the ground, twitching and flailing wildly.

"Phylum: Arthropoda, class: Insecta, and order: Blattodea!" Berna screamed.

A stampede of giant roaches slithered out of the dark. A terrible wind blew off the beating locusts' wings. It sounded like a fleet of helicopters had surrounded the house, blasting an earsplitting siren.

Skreeer-reeer-reeeee!

"Liz, weapons room!" I shouted, pointing down the corridor. "Have Kevin carry up as much gear as he

236

can. Victor, stay on me. Berna, hey, Berna! We have to protect Theo. We guard this door, okay?"

Berna was trembling. She still had the needle in her hand. I was worried she would fall and jab herself in the eye with it.

"Someone needs to take the antidote," I said. I rolled up my sleeve. "Do it."

"But–" Victor said.

"There's no time. Now!" I screamed and closed my eyes.

A sharp jab stuck my arm. OW-ZERS! Searing, fiery liquid burned under my skin. It brought tears to my eyes. Berna capped the needle. "Not so bad."

I gave her a watery smile. My stomach suddenly lurched into my throat. The room spun in great big swoops. I tried to stand, but I was too dizzy. I slumped on the couch.

This might have been a bad idea, I thought.

I was woozy, and my hands were jelly. My fingers had swollen to the size of plump sausages. Everything was in slow motion.

"Serena found us. I don't know how, but she found us," Liz said, shaking her head.

I managed to peer outside. Fear shot through me.

Serena stood in our garden in all her spider glory. Her fourth leg stabbed the ground, and her third leg rubbed against it, raking across the exoskeleton of her lanky shin, creating a horrific shrieking noise like the mating call of a thousand cicadas or the grating love song of a giant cricket.

Serena's song pierced the fog and soil.

"You are trespassing!" Wugnot shouted into the PA system. "By the Order of the Rhode Island Baby-sitters, stop what you are doing and lay down your weapons."

Her legs fiddled faster. The song grew louder. The earth trembled and bulged.

"Kevin, hand me that crossbow!" Liz screamed.

Frost on the ground crackled and split as wiry feelers rose from the depths of the garden. More roaches—*joy!*—clawed their way up from the dirt, shaking the soil from their enormous shells, skittering dutifully in response to the queen's song.

Serena smiled, welcoming those in her dominion, and gave them orders to attack.

THWACK! An arrow thunked between a roach's eyes. Liz lowered her crossbow.

"There's too many to be using arrows!" I shouted.

But it came out like "Gaaaaaaboooooo!"

I groaned and shook my head, trying to focus on the blurs around me.

"Get it together, Ferguson!" Liz snapped.

Berna shined her flashlight into my pupils. "Just hang in there."

I felt fingers take my hand.

It was Victor. He was holding me up.

"I got you," he said. I leaned on him, one thought cutting through the haze: *Don't you dare throw up in front of him.*

In the security booth, Wugnot slammed down a large brass switch with a huge red handle. A low electric hum trembled through the walls. The lights in the living room flickered. A wired perimeter outside the cottage glowed bright blue as power surged through it, wrapping the house in crackling electricity, just as the swarm reached it.

The house shuddered as each insect exploded against the perimeter's shield, splattering the house in gloopy guts.

"I got the shutters!" Liz called out, sliding across the floor on her knees.

She roundhouse kicked a switch on the wall. Storm shutters rolled down over the windows, muffling the angry chirps and clicks and shrieks.

Victor slung my arm over his shoulder. Acid rose in my clenched throat. I went to speak, but instead I puked all over Victor's sneakers.

"Gross!" he yelled, kicking my sick off his shoes.

"Sorry 'bout your Jordans," I groaned.

I felt lighter. And I could talk.

I grabbed a sword from inside the Lone Wolf and

hacked at bug appendages.

"Get out of our house!" I screamed, filling the air with bug juice.

The power flickered. All the lights in the cottage died. Only the glow of Penelope the pixie's lantern-butt skittered across the walls.

"They bit through the power!" Wugnot announced as he handed out emergency flashlights.

"Protect the turtle!" I kept shouting.

WHAM! The door to the lab flung open. Dawn, big-eyed and crazed, glared from the doorway. Tubes stuck out of her arms and nose, and her spider bite looked like a shrunken purple volcano.

"The queen has arrived!" she screamed. Cackling wildly, Dawn sprinted toward the nursery. With bizarre strength, she threw back the cabinet and wrenched open the door. Baby Theo cried as his bonkers mother hovered over his crib.

"Come and meet the queen," Dawn whispered to her child.

I shoved Dawn aside and scooped up the little chunklet. Baby Theo stopped crying. His giant round eyes locked on me.

"Adooooo," said Theo. I took that to mean "thanks."

Foam bubbled in the corners of Dawn's mouth. "Give . . . me . . . my . . . BABY!"

She lunged, but I pushed her out of the room and kicked the door closed in her face. Her fists pounded on the nursery door as Victor and Berna held it closed.

"What's that sound?" Berna asked.

Beneath the shrieking and hammering of the insects, a high-pitched, airy whistle played a twisted harmony. It was an organ grinder. The kind they used to play at fairgrounds and creepy, old-timey circuses. The tune was so happy and merry it made me sick.

If you go down to the woods today, you're sure of a big surprise. . . .

The monster bugs grew still, and soon all that we heard was the chilling *toot-toot* of the carnival music.

If you go down in the woods today, you'd better go in disguise!

I braved a glance through the slats of one of the storm shutters. . . .

Because today's the day the teddy bears have their piiiiiiiicnic!

A spectacled man stood at the start of the gravel driveway, cranking the handle of a wooden music box full of bellows and tall brass pipes on wheels.

"Professor Gonzalo's Wonder Harmonium" was embossed in gold letters on the front.

"Professor Gonzalo!" I said under my breath. "One of the Seven."

241

"Oh gosh, oh man, this is nuts," Berna mumbled.

Seeing the fear in Berna's eyes filled me with dread. She's usually the chilled-out, smart one. If she was freaked, we were *def* in trouble.

Liz cocked her head and listened to the creepy ditty being played by the awful mad Professor who was dressed like an academic undertaker.

"Why is that freak playing that music?" she said.

Kevin began panting. Heaving for breath. His eyes glowed bright silver in the darkness.

"What's wrong with him?" Victor said quietly.

A low, unnatural growl rumbled in the beast boy's throat like a dog about to attack.

The organ's tempo grew faster. The chubby Professor sang along.

Dee-DOOT! Dee-DOOT! Dee-DOOT!

Kevin's paws grabbed at his long, floppy ears, and he let out an agonized wail. Liz dropped everything and ran to comfort him. "Kev, what's wrong?"

He roared in her face, stopping her in her tracks.

Dee-DOOT! Dee-DOOT! Dee-DOOT!

Hackles raised, the eight-foot-tall furball snarled through his tusks and turned on me.

I ran, but Kevin caught the back of my shirt. My feet pedaled the air as the monster dangled me, swiping at Baby Theo. Berna, Liz, and Victor pulled at Kevin's arms, but he swung his elbows, sending them

242

flying across the room.

"Kev, chill out!" I screamed, kicking at him.

The beast tossed me aside and smashed Victor into the wall. Kevin pried open my arms, plucking the newborn with his paws. Theo wailed, red in the face.

"Turtle!" I shrieked.

Kevin hurtled down the hall toward the front door, Theo in his arms.

"Stop right there, boyo." Wugnot stepped out from the security booth, cracking his knuckles.

The hobgoblin casually removed his trucker hat and tossed it aside before titling his nubby horn at the woolly freight train. Kevin charged in battering position.

"Brace for impact."

Their horns collided. The house shook. The monsters grunted, eye to eye. But Kevin was bigger, meaner, and younger, and with a powerful twist, Wugnot was sent tumbling aside, skidding across the floor, where he stayed.

"Wuggie!"

Poor Wuggie was out for the count.

Kevin's big foot booted open the front door. Theo wailed as Kevin carried him out into the night.

"No, no, no!" Liz screamed. "Kev, don't you dare!"

The hairy mutant looked back at Liz with torture in his eyes.

"Bullgarth," called Serena. "Come."

Serena's presence and the Professor's call broke him. Kevin sprinted toward them with Baby Theo. We chased after them, but the doorway suddenly filled with enormous locusts and supersized roaches, and we were caught inside a blizzard of bugs. We retreated back into the house as they smashed through the halls, ripped open doors, ate through the wood.

Through the swarm, I saw Kevin—with an obedient expression on his dumb, hairy face—kneel in the snow at Serena's side, holding Theo as the Professor played that hideous tune. Kevin offered his prize to his queen.

Serena took Baby Theo from Kevin and held him aloft as she looked up at him.

"My, aren't you hideous," sneered Serena, holding the child at arm's length. "Think you're going to grow up big and strong and destroy the Boogey family, do you? Not if I have anything to say about you, you dirty, rotten thing."

Baby Theo was crying so much, tears dropped from

his eyes. Seeing that poor little chunk so scared and afraid made my blood surge.

"No!" I darted toward them.

In the distance an alarm bell rang. My eyes widened.

"The monster stables. They opened the stables," I gasped.

The Grunk, the Blue-Bone Sizzler, the Brush Troll, and the Oozer were out and headed toward the house. They smashed through the storm shutters. Everything in the cottage shattered and broke.

"Fall back!" Liz shouted above the noise.

The Grunk bashed in the nursery room door. Amid the wreckage, Dawn cried out happily as a cluster of locusts picked her up, talons holding her by her Olive Garden uniform. Their wings beat furiously, and Dawn was lifted off the ground.

"I'm ready, my queen!" she laughed.

She looked like a zealot hovering in the sky.

"Let go of her!" Berna jumped, grabbed Dawn's legs, and tried to pull her down. More locusts attached to Berna, swinging her up into the air.

"Kelly!" Berna shrieked, reaching out, vanishing into the cloud of locusts.

I reached for her, but a Blue-Bone Sizzler stomped in my path. Its cheeks puffed up, filling with noxious gas. I narrowed my eyes, trying to remember a funny detail I had read about the Sizzler's gas. . . .

The blue monster spun around and aimed its butt at me.

Oh, right. It doesn't shoot fire out of its mouth. It shoots it out of its—

BOOM!

A stinky fireball burst from the creature's crack. The heat was like a searing force field. Flames spread across the walls.

BOOM! Another flaming gas cloud caught the ceiling on fire. That stinker skipped into the library, filled both its cheeks, and blasted our beautiful, towering bookshelves with farts aflame. Fiery pages fell like giant red snowflakes.

Emergency sprinklers came on, but it was too late. We were choking in the rolling black smoke that filled the halls. The roaches scattered in the light of the rising fire, while the locusts were oddly drawn toward it.

"Look out!" screamed Victor as the ceiling began to collapse in great chunks all around us. We were trapped in a raging bonfire.

Explosions shook from deep within the basement.

"The teddy bear bombs!" Liz shouted, tackling Victor and me to the ground as screaming jets of flames broke through the floor.

"This way!" shouted Liz, opening the cabinet of a grandfather clock.

247

I grabbed our backpacks and Liz pulled Victor and me inside the clock as the ceiling caved in behind us. We tumbled down a long, spiral metal slide that spat us into a cramped concrete tunnel. Liz flicked on a flashlight and ran down the dark, dusty corridor.

"What is this?" I asked, following quickly.

"Sitters built it in 1952 as a bomb shelter. Escape hatch is up here," she said.

The ceiling shuddered above us, raining dust on our heads as Liz climbed up a metal ladder. I stopped to catch my breath, poison churning in my veins.

Through the cracks between the bricks, I could see outside, where Serena was shooting a sticky web around Berna and Wugnot, cocooning them until they were trapped in her spider swaddle. Poor Berna. She looked horrified.

Liz, Victor, and I poked our heads out of the grass-camouflaged trapdoor like frightened gophers. Headquarters was ablaze. Fire poured from the windows, engulfing the fairy-tale roof. Carnival-masked trolls danced with glee around the flames as they handed their queen the portrait of her they had stolen. The Spider Queen blew her pretty painting a kiss as they strapped it to the roof of the Rolls.

Professor Gonzalo packed up his Wonder Harmonium and snapped a metal collar around Kevin's neck as the beast obediently bowed his head. Serena took the chain and yanked it.

"I knew you'd come to your senses," she sneered.

Head hung low, Kevin let out a sad wail.

"I trained you better than that, Bullgarth!" spat the sweating Professor, shoving the harmonium into Kevin's paws. "I'm taking you back to the island after this. Someone needs another lesson."

Cradling Theo, Serena dragged Kevin into her black Rolls-Royce. She looked back at the crackling fire and smiled wickedly.

"Good job leading us here, Bullgarth," said Serena.

Liz gasped beside me.

"Your brother is a hairy double agent!" I said.

Bullgarth—I mean Kevin—glanced in the direction of our voices. We ducked down. His eyes shimmered. I knew he could see us. We held our breaths. Would Kevin give us up?

The escaped monsters circled Serena, awaiting their orders. "What about the other babysitters?" the Professor asked.

"They'll come to us," said Serena. She looked at the gorgeous, shivering baby in her arms. "Right now, all I want is to do is feed."

34

Tears streamed from my eyes. I was paralyzed with fear and heartache. In utter shock, Victor looked at me. Ashes and snow fell between us. He couldn't believe it. None of us could.

The bad guys had won.

"This can't be happening," I whispered.

I looked to Liz, but she was entranced by the horrific fire, her tear-filled eyes glistening in the red glow. Our home was gone forever. Hundreds of years of history and memories burned into flames. The crest of the babysitters toppled and vanished into the heat and smoke.

My insides felt hollow and dead. I had failed. Madame Moon was right. My best was not nearly good enough. I felt like I was drowning. I'd failed. I was a failure. Time to face facts.

It's like the Mighty Kang said: the little turtle will bring peace to the world of sun and air.

I blinked. *Wait a minute.* Maybe we did have a chance.

I ran off into the woods. Liz and Victor followed.

"Mighty Kang!" I shouted. "I call upon you!"

If anyone can help us, a nine-hundred-year-old Cloud Serpent can.

The waterfall was a cascade of rippling, bitter frost. A trout tail jutted from the ghostly, icy falls. I squinted into the brackish freeze. The creek behind the cottage had frozen over. The Mighty Kang was trapped in a block of ice behind the waterfall.

Major gut punch. The Might Kang was frozen. Vee was gone. Cassie, Curtis. Berna, Wugnot. Dawn. My parents. And the handsome little turtle. Baby Theo. I knew Victor and Liz were with me, but I felt strangely alone.

"What do we do?" Victor asked.

I saw Victor's and Liz's faces. They were just as scared and defeated as me. Liz had found her brother only to lose him again. Victor no longer thought it was cool to be a babysitter. He understood the stakes and danger, and it gave him a defeated look in his eyes.

I once read about these kinds of moments in the *Babysitter's Guide to Monster Hunting:*

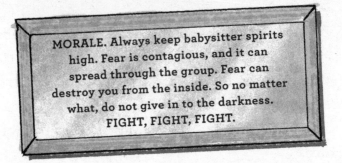

I knew if I fell apart, they would fall apart, and if we were going to save the sitters and the adorable chunklet-turtle, we had to keep going.

If Mama Vee were here, what would she say? Probably something annoying like "Believe in yourself, Kelly. You have trained for this."

My eyes narrowed. I have trained for this.

"Okay, everyone," I said, lifting my chin. "Weapons check."

We knelt and showed the contents of our babysitter backpacks.

Victor emptied his pockets.

I put my hands on my hips. Pretty measly weapons if we were going to confront a house full of monsters.

A good babysitter is resourceful.

"When life gives you lemons, go kill monsters with lemons," I said. "Let me see your hands, Victor."

I took Victor's hands and wrapped duct tape around his knuckles with the sticky side up. I broke open the packet of Legos and stuck the red and blue bricks onto the tape. Victor clenched his fists with his Lego-

252

studded knuckles. I held his hand for a lingering moment, but his fingers were cold and shaking. Victor quickly pulled away. I looked at my own hands. They weren't shaking at all. Weird.

"Almost midnight, and we need to get to Hargrave Manor before Serena performs her ritual on Theo."

"What ritual?" Victor asked.

"Check the guide," Liz and I replied in unison.

From Kelly Ferguson's copy
of A Babysitter's Guide to Monster Hunting:

RITUALS

(This entry is for spells and ceremonies
involving newborns. For Rituals involving
toddlers, adults, or animals, see page 564.)

FUN FACT: A haunted or holy/unholy site, such
as a cemetery or a haunted house, can be a
great source for spiritual vortex power, which
is needed to perform such rituals. The more
evil the spirits present, the stronger the
tether.

TIME REQUIRED: The ritual takes about thirty
minutes for full transfer.

**FOR FURTHER READING, SEE MONSTER
CEREMONIES/HOLIDAYS ENTRIES FOR:** Day of
the Dead, Samhain, All Hallows Eve, Krampusmas,
the winter solstice, the Ides of March, Asp
Wednesday, Friday the 13th aka "Caa-caa-caa
Chaa-chaa-chaa Day", Valentine's Day, St. Agnes

Eve, Shrovetide, Beltane, the Day of Bonfires, Children's Day, and the Lake George Monster Fourth of July Family Picnic

NOTE: This can be a very disturbing, life-changing event for most sitters.

HOW TO BREAK THE RITUAL: Once the psychic tether is made and the life force drainage begins, little can be done to stop the flow of life and youth from child to monster. Interfering might result in harm or serious damage to you or the subject. Best-case scenario: your hair will turn white. Just ask Mama Vee.

The initiator must be stopped first by a possible psychic power surge, which might kill the victim. A mirror blessed by a holy man can be used to trick the connection into thinking it is still intact, but this is a crude method and can result in residual effects (see Double, Double, Toil and Whoops My Fault on page 139).

Just grabbing the kid and running away is not an option. Precautions must be taken. Break the spell, or it will break you.

"I hate rituals," Liz said, walking to her dirt bike. "I'll ride my bike and you—"

Whoomph! The front of the house collapsed in a flaming heap onto her motorcycle. The gas tank caught, and I yanked Liz away just before it exploded.

"Are you freaking kidding me?" Liz screamed. "It took me four hundred babysitting jobs to buy that thing!"

Ding-a-ling!

My ears zeroed in on a sound just above the crackling, snapping flames.

Dinka-dinka-dink!

It sounded like bells. Tiny, magical.

"Penelope!" I screamed, and bolted toward the fire.

The faint chimes cried for help from deep within the blaze. I grabbed a fallen wooden beam that had rolled free from the fire, and jammed it under the crushed roof, trying to get enough leverage. Liz and Victor joined me, and together, the three of us lifted the flaming, white-hot beam.

A golden streak shot from the flames.

DING-A-DING!

The sewers. "That's how we we're sneaking in?" I asked, repulsed.

Penelope *bing-bing-bing*ed like a winning slot machine as Liz drove the busted babysitter mobile into the land of mansions: the Vandersnuff Summer Palace, the Gilded Frog Château, the Great Goldberg Estate.

Penelope told us how Mama Vee had fallen into a chamber of webs in the basement of Hargrave Manor. Vee sent Penelope from her pocket to come and get us. (Luckily, Liz speaks Pixie, so she interpreted.) There was a secret entrance through the drains.

"Kevin told me about a drainpipe," Liz said, staring through the windshield.

"Are you sure we can trust him?" I said.

Liz clenched her jaw. "That music's what made him go crazy. Professor Gonzalo's a smart, sick dude. He controls Kevin with his harmonium. And I am going to bash the monster geek's face right in."

We approached the hulking horror of Hargrave Manor. Except for the shining ice ringing its crooked towers, the weathered, bleak mansion was barely visible against the backdrop of night. We parked and climbed in through the twisted iron fence.

"I say we run the Haunted House play," I whispered.

"Nice thinking, newb," Liz agreed with a nod.

"Haunted House play?" asked Victor.

I tossed him the guide.

Quiet and swift, we snuck tigerlike through the dead weeds sprouting up through the frost. I saw the faint outline of sneakers, barely visible beneath the freshly fallen snow.

"Cassie and Curtis have been this way," I said.

Finding those tracks wasn't dumb luck.

"They tried the same maneuver," I mumbled.

And look what happened to them.

I held up my fist. Victor and Liz stopped. "Slight change of plans," I said. "Follow me."

I lead the group through a crumbling stone gate to the frozen shrubs of a long, dead garden at the side of the house. Hidden among the twisting thorns, bronze children were trapped in time, each posed in play. One little statue-child was flying a bronze kite that hung in the air, dripping with icicles.

Penelope clinked loudly for us to stop at the edge of an enormous stone fountain with a broken Egyptian obelisk in the center. Its shattered tip looked like a lethal, ancient spear, hewn from rock with the sole purpose of killing a giant. The recon pixie found a drain in the bottom of the fountain.

We reached down and, together, pried open the small grate. Before entering the belch-reeking pipes, Penelope fluttered up to us and gave us each a kiss on the nose for good luck. My face was so cold I barely felt the pixie's kiss, but it was good to know it was there.

"Victor, follow me. Liz, bring up the rear."

Liz grabbed my shoulder. "Quit being brave for your boyfriend, newb," she whispered.

"Theo's my responsibility," I said, ducking down. "And stop calling me 'newb.' This isn't my first rodeo."

"Okay, tough guy." Liz smirked. "Show us how it's done."

Roots wormed down through cracks. Penelope sat on my backpack and held my flashlight since her lantern-butt still wasn't 100 percent. I shimmied my way in, slowly scooting forward. I had a horrible feeling of being facedown in a coffin. Deeper we went, and I felt the enormous weight above us.

If there is an earthquake, we'll be flattened like pancakes. We'll be stuck down here, buried forever under tons of earth. Stop thinking of that stuff, Kelly! Focus on the light at the end of the tunnel.

"My leg! Something's got my leg!" Victor suddenly screamed and kicked his legs.

A squeal ran over my jeans and across my jacket. My back arched as a wet rat burrowed through my hair and ran off ahead of us. Penelope jabbed after its leathery tail.

"False alarm," Victor sighed. "Just a rat."

"Keep it together, dude," Liz whispered.

"It's his first rodeo, Liz," I called back. "Give him a break."

Deeper along, the pipe split. Left or right. Penelope rang and pointed her dagger to the left tunnel, which was slicked with frozen moss and strands of green scum-sicles circled by clouds of gnats.

"Yucky," I whispered.

There was an echoing scurry in front of me, and I froze. Victor bumped into my sneakers.

"Something's up there," I murmured.

I breathed faster, the tunnel crushing the wind from my lungs. The face of a giant cockroach caught in our flashlights. It shrieked, clacking its mandibles. Penelope was snatched up by its feelers and pulled into its mouth.

Shink! The little pixie drove her dagger right between its eyes. The monster roach squealed and thrashed its head. I flicked my wrist and pierced under its shell, right behind the roach's neck. Its head fell at an odd angle, and its whole body went limp.

"Nice shot, Pen," I said.

Now I just had to push the dead roach in front of me while shimmying up the tunnel. I shoved the hideous giant creeper out of the drainpipe and slithered out behind it into a bleak basement. Mason jars, filled with odd floating foods, lined the shelves.

"A canning room," Liz whispered.

We quietly crept past rows of dusty jars filled with strange pickled meats and moldy fruits. A crooked wooden staircase (it's always a crooked wooden staircase, isn't it?) rose to meet a door that seemed to hover in the darkness. Everything was still and silent.

This felt too easy. Serena was smart. She knew we would come.

I've been expecting you, child, the dark door seemed to croak. *We have chocolates and peppermints and treacle tarts and gumdrops delight. All waiting for you, silly children. Enter my web.*

36

Frescoes peeled away from the walls. The smell of rotted earth and decay filled my nose. Clouds of gnats buzzed around us, choking the air.

I tucked Penelope into my jacket breast pocket, our chests heaving against each other. She pointed us toward the end of the hallway, where an elegant chandelier was smashed across the floor.

"Stay close to the walls and keep to the shadows," I whispered.

We passed giant double doors that leaned on their rusty hinges. In the crooked space between the doors, I saw figures standing perfectly still. I slipped back tightly, signaling Victor and Liz: "Stop, someone's in there."

Liz stuck out her phone, stretched it through the crack in the doors, and snapped a picture. Tucked into the shadows behind a broken cabinet, we looked at the picture and gasped.

Officer Muntz. Sheriff Heep. My neighbors. Hundreds of people.

Penelope shot into the room, and her tiny glow illuminated faces with their eyes closed, as if they were sleeping on their feet. It looked like a mannequin warehouse.

"Dad?" Liz gasped.

I tried to stop her, but she pulled the large brass door handle and swept inside, weaving between the motionless people. Victor and I watched, horrified from the doorway as Liz walked up to her father, Hank. He was in his robe. His eyes were closed. He was breathing, his large gut rising and falling under his T-shirt and flannel, but his lower lip was protruding, as if he was a baby in a deep sleep.

"He's been bit," said Liz. I saw the two red bite marks on the side of his neck.

"Keep watch," I whispered to Victor.

He nodded, and I stepped into the cursed ballroom and cautiously moved around the frozen mob, past my neighbors, the police, a random Amazon delivery guy—even my algebra teacher, Mr. Flogger. (Though if I'm honest, from the way Mr. Flogger would smirk when he assigned us two hours' worth of homework, I always suspected him of being an evil, brainwashed lizard.) All with spider bites on their jugular veins.

Serena had spread her eight-legged babies across my town and had infected nearly everyone I knew.

No wonder Serena was always on the front lines

of every war and giant tragedy. She probably used her puppets to start them, just so she could get rich or spread evil monster hate. And now, she was going to use my poor town to start her next wave of horror across the world.

No way. Not on my watch.

Liz looked at her father's peaceful face, and tears glistened in her eyes. She reached out and gently touched his stubbly cheek.

I went to pull her away when I saw my parents standing among the lifeless mob. (Mom, Dad, if you're reading this, I am soooo sorry. And also you shouldn't be reading this because it's my private property.)

Dawn was also there, and almost lifeless in her Olive Garden uniform. Tammy and Deanna and the Princess Pack were there, too. Their thick makeup looked like pretty masks.

"¡Mamá!" Victor cried, leaving his post at the hallway and bolting inside.

His whole family was there. Even his grandmother. Victor fell to his knees before his family.

"Wake up!" he cried.

"Victor," I said. "Not so loud . . ."

"Wake up, Mamá!"

"Victor, stop!" Liz hissed.

Grandma Madrina's eyes snapped open. She had a

wicked, Cheshire cat grin on her face. "Bow down to the queen!" she shrieked.

Everyone's eyes began to open. It was like watching a horrific domino effect of flashing eyeballs. I grabbed Victor and pulled him away. Liz sprinted away from her father, who was swiping the air behind her. "I love the queen! You will, too!"

Penelope swooped overhead, warning me to duck the grappling arms of Tammy and Deanna and the possessed princesses. "C'mon, K-Ferg, surrender!" screamed Tammy.

"Surrender!" screamed Victor's father.

"Surrender!"

Sneakers squeaking, we shot out from the ballroom and slammed the doors just as the stampede of people-puppets crashed into them. We pressed our backs against the buckling wood and planted our heels. Arms swiped through the crack. Snarling, angry neighbors growled.

"This is worse than Black Friday at Walmart," Liz said.

"Kelly, you stop this right now and surrender to the queen, young lady!" my mother yelled.

I saw a rusted iron curtain rod leaning against a window. I snatched it and shoved it through the door handles. *BAM! BAM!* The shaking doors held. The hinges squeaked and threatened to snap lose.

"Open these doors, Victor! We raised you better than this!" Grandma Madrina cried.

Victor crossed himself, disturbed.

"You will fail!" my mother screamed.

"I know you don't mean that, Mom!" I shouted back, trying to keep positive as we ran from the shuddering clatter of zombielike hands beating against the crooked doors.

In the great hall, two sweeping staircases curled up to the second floor like great horns. An enormous marble *H* was embedded in the floorboards. We spun around, searching the shadows, trying to listen above the insanity in the ballroom far behind us.

I tilted my head. Somewhere up above, Theo was crying. A nasty, guttural cry.

He needs his bottle, you monsters. He needs his diaper changed. He needs to be cuddled.

"Theo's upstairs," I whispered.

Ding-a-ding! Penelope chimed.

"Trapped in Serena's lair," Liz whispered. "With the others."

Victor moved toward the sweeping staircase. I grabbed his arm.

"Too obvious," I said. "She's expecting us to take the stairs. Find another way up."

We snuck into the rotted kitchen. Black mold crawled

up the walls. Victor found a small door in the wall near the pantry. He opened it and Penelope shined her butt-light up into the vaulted, empty dumbwaiter. We all jammed our heads inside.

"Yeah, this is much more sneaky," I said. "And disgusting."

Ding-a-ding! Penelope agreed.

"How are we going to get up there?" Victor whispered. "You have a rope?"

Remember Heck Weekend? How to climb without ropes . . .

"We're going to free-climb," I said. "Watch."

I pulled myself all the way inside and pushed against the chute walls with my hands and feet. I shimmied up slowly. Just like I had learned. Liz and Victor followed suit. The termite-riddled wood crumbled under our grip as we climbed up inside it.

We spilled into a second-floor hallway, where shutters clattered in the icy blizzard howling off the ocean.

"Where to now?" Victor asked, peering across to closed wooden doors.

All we could hear was the quaking, storm-pounded walls. I wiped my sweaty palms on my jeans. Terrified, Penelope zipped back into my pocket.

"This place is enormous," Liz said. "They could be anywhere."

Something slippery squished under Victor's sneaker.

"Dees-gusting!" he said, hopping around, looking at the bottom of his shoe.

Liz rolled her eyes. "Smooth move, newb number two."

"Wait!" I said, stopping Victor from scraping his sneaker. "Let me see."

"What's to see? It's dookie," he said.

"The correct term is 'scat,'" I said as I inspected the muck. "The texture, the shape . . ."

"Spare me the details," said Liz.

I opened my guide to the Scat Chart I copied from Berna, and cross-checked it with the caca on the floor.

"This is Kevin's all right," I said. "It's fresh, too."

"You can say that again," Victor moaned. "Can I wipe my shoe now?"

"Yes. And thank you for asking," I said.

I spotted a second dung heap down a corridor in the east wing. "Follow that poo!"

We ran to doo-doo number two and looked around. The wall behind us buckled. A huge crack broke the plaster. And then I heard the sickeningly sweet, pied piper organ music of Professor Gonzalo.

Dee-DOOT! Dee-DOOT! Dee-DOOT!

The wall caved in like rotted bark. In a thunder of horns and drywall, Kevin tumbled out into the hall-way, furiously shaking his head. Liz lassoed her rope around his horns and pulled tight. Kevin thrashed, sending his sister hurtling around the hallway.

"I got you, Liz!" I yelled, grabbing the rope.

Victor took hold too, and the three of us were yanked off our feet as Kevin thundered down the corridor. Wall lights shattered against his horns.

"Kevin, cut it out!" Liz screamed.

Dee-DOOT! Dee-DOOT! Dee-DOOT! The music grew louder at the Professor emerged from one of the rooms far behind us, cranking his Wonder Harmonium.

Liz looked back at the spectacled, sweaty round man.

"Hang on to him, newb," Liz said to me. "I'll be right back!"

"Stop calling me 'newb'!"

"Stop acting like one!" I heard Liz cry as she released the rope.

"She always has to get the last word," I growled.

Looking back, I saw Liz charge toward the Professor. Gonzalo calmly swung open a door. An explosion of locusts and cockroaches filled the hall with their chilling shriek: *skreeeer-reeee-reee!*

"Gonzalo!" screamed Liz.

Relentless, she charged toward the man who had turned her brother into a monster. No way was she backing down. She became pure love and vengeance in a single body, swooping her blades through the storm of insects.

Bug heads rolled.

"Yeah, LeRue!" I shouted over my shoulder as Kevin dragged us down the hall.

"Uh, Kelly?" said Victor, staring ahead.

There was an explosion of colored glass. Rainbow shards flew around me. Kevin and I plunged forward, toppling out of the window. Victor had let go of the rope.

But me? I hit a slanted section of the roof and slid uncontrollably down the shingles.

"This is bad, very bad!" I yelled.

My fingers clutched on to the rain gutter. My legs danced in the wind. The broken obelisk was fifty feet below me. Its jagged tip like a rocky dagger waiting to kabob me.

"Kelly!" I heard Victor yell from inside the shattered window.

At least he was smart enough to let go of the rope.

Kevin's claws scraped against the shingles like a scared dog. The gutter groaned under my grip. Kevin howled and scrambled up the incline, perching on it like a gargoyle as he stared down at me, his head tilted in confusion about whether to let me live or die.

The gutter sprang loose from the brick, spilling snow and muck down my sleeves. I shrieked, ice and sludge pouring down my shirt as I hung over that horrific drop. The sharp metal point of the obelisk beneath my feet waited patiently to run me through. Penelope leapt from my pocket and tried to help me up, but she was too tiny to lift me up.

"I'm coming to get you!" Victor called.

"Don't! It's too slippery. That's an order!"

Dee-DOOT! Dee-DOOT! Dee-DOOT!

"Babysitter Bop! Hiyaaa!" I heard Liz scream from inside.

There was the sound of shattering pipes and breaking wood. The awful circus music stopped dead.

Crouching over me, Kevin shook his donkey ears, as if the buzzing in his brain had stopped.

Victor climbed out the window. Monster Kev scratched the air at him. Victor recoiled, skidded, and caught the edge of the window.

"Victor!" I cried. "I told you not to come out here!"

"Don't yell at me!" Victor shouted. "I'm being nice!"

"Well, now we're both going to die!"

My fingers slipped free. I dropped.

A warm, fuzzy paw grabbed my wrist, and I was yanked to a stop, my sneakers swaying just above the jagged statue. Lightning flashed in the sky. Looking up, I saw Kevin's snout sniff down at me. He held my fate in his paw, and I had a really bad feeling he was going to choose poorly.

I saw Liz emerge from the shattered window and carefully step onto the roof.

"Move it, Victor," Liz said.

She approached her brother with something in her hand. Hunched over, the monster wailed as she reached out and jammed her headphones into his donkey ears. Superloud, hard punk rock blasted into his ears. Kevin's silvery eyes awakened. He looked down at me.

"Please, please, please, please," I pleaded.

He hoisted me up and over the ledge, setting me gently inside the corridor. The Kevin we knew and loved, the big dumb bigfoot, was back.

Liz embraced her brother. He barked as she removed the lasso from his horns. Penelope rang out happily. We helped Victor inside; both of us were shivering.

At the end of the hall, Professor Gonzalo had staggered to his feet, holding himself up against the wall. He looked at his broken harmonium and scowled.

"You broke my machine!" the Professor sneered. "You wicked children!"

Kevin zeroed in on the pudgy Boogeyman and snarled. He scraped his paws against the floor, as if he were a bull about to charge. Liz took hold of his horns and held on tight to his back.

"Fetch," she said, pointing at the Boogeyman.

Kevin thundered toward the Professor. The little man blew into a dog whistle, but Kevin couldn't hear it. He had his headphones tucked into his ears, blasting drums and bass that provided a hard-core soundtrack for his charge.

"Now, now, Kevin," mumbled the Professor, adjusting his shattered glasses with an apologetic tone. "I was always good to you!" The mad genius screamed, running down the decayed hall.

Kevin bucked Professor Gonzalo into the air, tearing a hole in his pants and sending him smashing into the ceiling then crashing down to the ground. The Professor crawled desperately toward a doorway.

Kevin snorted and planted his giant foot in the sniveling Boogeyman's back.

"I can help you. Change you back," the Professor squealed.

Kevin barked, curious. He gruffly thumped his chest, as if to say, *You can do that?*

The Professor's shaking hands wiped his goatee, and he smiled cravenly. "Yes! If you let me go, I'll bring you to my island, and we can run some tests. I have potions and machines that can help you."

Kevin wailed at Liz. Liz looked at her brother's big hairy face, his tusks, and his deep-set silvery eyes.

"I love my brother the way he is," she said.

Kevin roared in agreement and raised his furry paw over the frightened Professor's face. The desperate Boogeyman flung himself back against the wall and pulled a hidden handle. The wall spun around, taking the Professor into the depths of Hargrave Manor. His laughter echoed through the walls as he vanished from sight, escaping the wrath of the LeRue siblings.

"Coward!" screamed Liz.

I trained my ear on the muffled cackle of the Professor as it wound through a hidden chamber behind the wallpaper. I signaled Kevin and pointed to a spot on the wall. Kevin smashed his giant paw through the plaster. In a burst of dust and crumbling wood, he dragged the Professor out of his secret passageway and thumped him onto the ground, planting his foot on the pathetic man's trembling chest.

"No one escapes the babysitters," I said, standing over him. "Now, where's the baby?"

The Professor pursed his lips

"Kev, rip his head off," I said. Kevin roared again and grabbed the Professor.

"U-upstairs," the Professor stuttered. "Third door on the left."

Penelope rang out a warning cry. Paws thumped down the second-floor hallway. The carnival-masked trolls bounded from the shadows. They looked like the staff of a very fancy hotel had dressed up a bunch of rabid chimpanzees and then set them lose.

Liz cracked her knuckles. "You and lover boy and the lightning bug find the queen," she said. "Me and Kev will hold these monkeys off."

As I picked up my sword from the ground, the deranged Professor chuckled. "Try all you want, little girl. You'll never defeat the queen! She has eight legs. You have two. She is immortal, monster royalty. You are a thirteen-year-old girl. You're not good enough, and you never will be!"

I tried to think of a cool comeback that would make me sound tough, but deep down, I knew the Professor was right. But my best would have to do.

Shafts of moonlight beamed through the wooden slats on the third floor. I crept with Victor toward two giant doors. I looked back at him. He was crossing himself, mumbling.

"Game time," I whispered. "You ready?"

"If I say I'm scared, does that make me a wimp?"

"It makes you normal. I'm terrified."

"Good," he said. "Well, not good, but you know what I mean."

I slapped the hilt of the silver dagger in his palm and closed his fist around the grip.

I put my finger to my lips as I knelt and peered through the keyhole.

I saw banners of thick spiderwebs crisscrossing the darkness.

"Stay low," I whispered, "and follow me."

We entered the massive room filled top to bottom with ghostly, shimmering threads. Penelope's light danced through the webbing, as if it were a chandelier. The design was impeccable, like some kind of fancy-pants jeweler had crafted it.

"Whoa," said Victor. But in a bad way.

"Eeeeeeooo!" cried Theo.

We found Theo swaddled in spider silk, suspended in a giant cobweb altar. He was crying up at the electric blue mist circling above him that looked as if it was trying to form a connection with his heart. There were fifty feet of sticky webs that separated us from Theo. I wanted to cross it, but I had to be careful.

"Where's Serena?" I whispered, looking up into the towering lair.

A slimy gurgle, like a jar of pudding caught in a vacuum cleaner, sounded on my right. The mushy Sleeknatch barreled toward us, its eyestalks flailing wildly.

"Ahhh!" Victor said.

"Don't think of it like a monster," I said. "Think of it like a soccer ball."

"I can do that." Victor reeled back and kicked the

meatball monster, sending it rolling across the floor.

He dribbled the Sleeknatch down the floorboards, driving forward like (insert famous soccer player's name here because I don't know any). The Sleeknatch wailed as it spun. Victor kicked it up onto his knee and bounced it up and down.

"Okay, now you're just showing off," I said. "We need to get Theo!"

Victor fired his toe into the Sleeknatch's side. The monster went airborne with the perfect kickoff. It shot wide, tumbling with great hang time toward the netting.

"Goal!" Victor shouted.

But the Sleeknatch bounced off the webbing like a trampoline and rocketed into Victor's head, knocking him back.

Victor stumbled and fell through a gaping hole in the floor behind him. I grabbed his hand, but he dragged me down with him. We tumbled into the darkness.

Good news: spiderwebs broke our fall.

Bad news: spiderwebs broke our fall.

Victor and I jerked to a bouncing stop in the echoing chamber, our arms and legs stuck in the gooey threads.

"I can't move," Victor said, struggling.

"Me neither," I said.

Even my hair was caught, and every time I lifted

my head, it felt like someone was pulling out strands of my hair. My eyes watered as I hung there, disoriented, immobile. I felt oddly weightless, suspended above a dark cavern.

"Sorry about that," Victor said. "I got carried away."

Sometimes boys are so dumb, I wanted to say. But I had to stay positive.

"Penelope," I whispered. "Can you move?"

A glow brightened from within my jacket, and she rang out. Penelope the pixie set to work hacking her tiny elfin dagger against the powerful silk. In the pixie's dancing light, I saw a box of Girl Scout cookies hanging from the threads. *Thin Mints*. A huge bite had been taken out of it.

"The Girl Scout Cookies play," I gasped. "They're down here."

I looked down to where the webs seemed to stretch forever.

"Penelope, shine down there," I whispered.

In the pixie's faint, golden lamp, I saw small sacs stuck to the webs like bunches of grapes. Thin, wiry limbs were curled together, floating in murky fluid.

"Spuh-spuh-spider eggs," I said.

Hundreds of them. Glistening, alive.

Don't faint. Don't throw up. Focus on your breathing! They're just eggs. Not spiders. Still, SUPERGAGGY.

A groan sounded beneath me. I craned my neck and saw Berna bound up and hanging upside down off a strand. She looked drained and pale.

"Bern! Are you okay?"

Berna groaned. "Fabulous."

Beside her, Wugnot, who was also wrapped up, hung like salami in the window of an Italian deli.

"Have you been bit?" Victor asked.

"No. But Serena fed on us," whimpered Berna.

"Musta taken a whole six-pack of blood from my veins," Wugnot moaned. "I'm beat."

Below them, on another tier of webbing, I saw a human-sized cotton-candy-ball wrapping around Mama Vee. Swaying below her in their own bundles of threads were Cassie and Curtis. I was elated to see their faces, even if they looked drained and unwell.

The gang's all here.

"They've been bit," Berna whispered. "Only a matter of time before they wake up under Serena's spell."

I thrashed angrily. "We gotta get out of here and get Theo."

"It's no use," said Wugnot. "Stuff's like quicksand. More you fight it, stronger it gets."

I looked at the web clinging to my jacket. It was like gum stuck to my sleeve, refusing to let go. I looked past the Lone Wolf sword dangling in the webs next to Victor, who was suspended beside me.

"Now do you see why I didn't want you coming?" I said.

"I'd do it again," said Victor.

I tried to reach out for his hand, but the gooey tendrils kept us apart.

"Well, aren't you two just the cutest," a chilling voice called from above.

Movement stirred the ghostly, shimmering threads. A dark shape floated toward us.

Serena dangled by her thread. She was in her element and excited.

"You don't know how long I've waited for this." Serena smiled, exposing her shining ivory fangs.

I gulped. She was enjoying this.

"At your service, Your Majesty," I said with a smirk.

She's not impressed. That was not cool or tough enough.

A moist, twisting noise curled in the shadows. Sacs of spider eggs peeled open. The wet legs of freshly hatched spiders writhed in the air.

"Yes, my children," cooed Serena. "It's time to feed."

"Eeeeeeeeo!" cried Theo above.

Serena's head jerked toward the ceiling. "Pardon me, I have a ritual to finish. I have to save the monster world from that wretched baby."

Serena ascended on her thread as spiders pattered up my jeans, their clawed feet pressing down against my jacket. We thrashed, but the webs held us tight.

"It's like having gum stuck in your hair," Victor cried.

Gum stuck in your hair . . . And how do you get gum out of your hair? I thought.

"Penelope," I whispered. "Reach into my pack and get the bottle of baby oil!"

A diligent ring chimed, and Penelope opened the zipper of my pack. The contents tumbled out, catching on the web like a freeze-frame. Penelope snagged the bottle and flew it up toward me, but it was too heavy for her to lift and she dropped it just above my head. The bottle hung upside down, just out of my reach.

"Hurry!" Berna cried out, kicking at the spiders crawling up her hands.

I strained, pulling against the stretchy sinews, my fingers just brushing the cap of the bottle of baby oil.

"Hustle it, Ferguson!" shouted Wugnot.

"No pressure," I said.

"Eeeee!" Victor's face was covered in spiders. The whites of his eyes stared at me through their legs, as if a big black hand were holding his face.

My index finger caught the top of the pink cap and flipped it open, spilling it down my arm. Doused in oil, I felt the web give way, and I tore my right arm free. I snatched the sword from its hovering snare and sliced at the spiders swarming up my chest, cutting them in half. I carved through the webs holding down my left arm, and I grabbed the baby oil, spraying it across my jeans.

"Mmmmffmm!" Victor cried out, his words muffled by the thorax on his mouth.

"Stay still!" I yelled.

I flicked the sword under the spider and flipped it like a pancake.

"*Gracias*," Victor gasped.

"I'm coming, Berna!"

I cut off a giant silvery thread and, clinging to it like a rope, swung down to Berna and Wugnot as I wildly chopped the attacking spiders. I doused Berna and Wugnot with oil, and they pulled the sticky lines from their hands.

"Babysitters, attack!" I cried.

Wugnot's tail snapped a cluster of spiders away. Berna kicked, sending the little beasties squealing.

Trapped in her webbed casing, Mama Vee glared up at us, her eyes alight with horror.

"Surrender to the queen!" screamed Vee.

In eerie synchronicity, Cassie and Curtis opened their eyes, tilting their upside-down heads so they could glare up at us too.

"Shhhhurrender!" screamed Cassie.

"The antidote," Berna said. "If only I had my tools, I could test your blood and see if—"

"We don't have time for that," I said. "Theo's up there. I have to save him before Serena drains his life force. Can you handle this?"

Berna nodded. "You know I can. Go get that baby."

I sheathed my sword behind my backpack and scaled the epic spiderweb, with Penelope lighting the way and Victor scrambling beside me.

At the top I caught a glimpse of Baby Theo, stuck in his cocoon, and Serena was circling him, chanting some strange tune. I signaled Victor to stop. I knew from science class that spiders detect the slightest vibration in their webs.

"I'll distract Serena," I whispered to Victor. "You grab Theo."

Victor looked at me with huge worried eyes. No time for pep talks.

"Wait for my signal," I said. "And I mean wait."

I ascended the web. When I was near Serena, I furiously shook the line. Serena's head snapped down at me. Her eyes narrowed into thin slits.

"Oh, Kelly," sighed Serena. "Why won't you just die?"

"Not my style," I said.

I snagged a dangling silk banner, and like I was springboarding with a bungee cord, I swung myself at her. Serena leaped forward, spiraling through her deadly weaves.

We flew through the air, hurtling toward each other.

Clang! My sword hit against the thick exoskeleton around her legs. Agile as a ballerina, Serena's claws shot out at me in a flurry. I could barely deflect them. It was like fighting a killer sewing machine.

"That's the best you can do?" Serena sighed again.

"Adaaaaa," I heard Baby Theo coo.

Across the chamber, Theo bounced happily in his cocoon as Victor cut the baby loose with a silver dagger. He was trying to shush Theo, but the little turtle was excited to be free.

"No!" shrieked Serena.

"Run, Victor!" I shouted.

Serena dove toward Victor. I swung down, sailing after her, like Tarzan on a silky vine.

Clutching Theo, Victor scrambled across the webs. Serena shot a jet of thread at him, catching him in the back. Victor flew like a yo-yo with Theo in his arms into Serena's clutches.

"Let us see if you taste as sweet as you look," she mused with a cackle.

39

Victor writhed, but Serena's threads looped around him tighter and tighter. I scrambled toward them. Serena locked eyes with me.

"Say good-bye," she sneered.

"Don't, please," I begged.

She sank her fangs into Victor's jugular vein.

"Victor!" I cried.

He shuddered and flopped in her clutches. As she filled him with toxic venom, she never broke eye contact with me. Victor's head slumped forward. I screamed, but nothing came out.

Serena plucked Baby Theo from his grasp.

In a rage, I hoisted my sword. But she blocked it

with her giant limbs. Theo wailed in her arms as she battled me in a graceful dance of death.

She swung from her thread like an evil Spider-Man. I grabbed a web and flung myself into the air, vaulting across the sweeping chamber. In midair, four of her legs kicked me in the stomach. I gasped and fell onto a single spider thread, barely able to keep my balance. I felt like a tightrope walker. Perched on a line, Serena stalked toward me. I noticed one of her legs was hanging limply, tucked behind her gown.

"You're good, Kelly," said Serena. "But not good enough. I can make you amazing."

She held out her hand sparkling with jewels.

"Never!" I screamed.

She shook the line, and I slipped back into the cavern, catching a thread and dangling over the echoing darkness as she stood over me. "Never say never, darling," she taunted.

"Surrender, Kelly," said Victor, feeling the pulsing spider bite on his neck. "We can finally be together. All of us. Just one big happy family."

"No, Victor," I cried. "Not you. Please not you."

Serena leaned down to my ear. "Your friends can't save you. Neither can your family. They all belong to me now."

She snapped her fingers. Across the spiderwebbed

chamber, the door flew open. Serena's masked trolls and Professor Gonzalo dragged Kevin and Liz inside. They were bound up in rusty iron shackles.

Serena smiled at my terrified face.

"Sorry, newb," Liz said with a shrug.

Kevin let out an apologetic roar.

"Quiet, you hideous little beast," said the Professor. "You are in for a lifetime of torture."

I struggled to hang on to the line, but my fingers were slipping. I lifted my arm to swing the sword, but Serena shot a glob of goo, knocking it from my hand. My only weapon was gone.

Serena held up the baby, showing him to me like a trophy.

"You see? You hold nothing. And I hold the world's greatest hope for destroying monsters. This little turtle. But I'm afraid his short little life is over."

Her fangs sizzled with delight as they sank toward the child's neck.

Ding-a-ding! Like a flying sparkler, Penelope flew toward Serena, bells screaming. The pixie had been tucked away, waiting for her moment of attack, her final chance at pixie resistance, and this was it. She flew, dagger aimed at Serena.

Without looking, Serena's hand shot out and grabbed the pixie in midair. I gasped as she glowed furiously in the Spider Queen's fist.

"Penelope!" I cried.

Serena took one look at the little pixie and then shoved her into her mouth, gobbling her up with one large swallow. *Crunch, crunch, crunch.*

My stomach seized. Serena chewed and felt around her mouth with her tongue before finally spitting out the tiny crooked dagger.

"You monster!" I screamed.

"I take that as a compliment," Serena said with a grin. "Soon you'll be just like everyone else. And you'll never worry if you're good enough or not. Because I will take wonderful care of all of you."

I heard the wail of the people trapped in the ballroom. My mother and father. I heard Mama Vee calling out to me down below with Cassie and Curtis. Berna and Wugnot howled at me too. They had all been bit.

"They are all under my dominion," said the Spider Queen. "And they will help me launch my greatest attack against humanity. My brother wanted an army of nightmares, but I now have an army of humans. And there is no better or more destructive force than that."

My breath felt heavy, as if a stone was sitting on my chest. The empty nothing feeling surrounded my every move.

I'm just a kid. Hardly a babysitter. She's taken everyone from me and turned them against me.

And now she's turning me against myself.

"There is no hope for you, Kelly Ferguson. It is time."

Hanging there, I was filled with horrible thoughts of giving up. My best was not nearly good enough.

"Okay," I said, bowing my head.

Serena seemed pleasantly surprised. "Okay?"

"Only if you promise to let Theo go," I said weakly.

Serena cackled. "I always keep my promises."

I leaned my neck out, offering it to her. Serena's eyes sparkled. At last she had me. Her legs hoisted me up, bringing me close to her pale, flawless skin.

I looked at Baby Theo, who was in the clutches of Serena's sixth leg. His beautiful eyes looked up at me with wonder and pure love.

"Adooo," whispered Baby Theo.

"Good-bye, little turtle," I whispered lovingly.

Serena's cold shadow loomed over me. I felt the sting of two sharp needles sinking into my skin. Her warm lips wiggled around my neck. I shivered as I felt her latch on and begin to draw my blood into her mouth. My heart skipped and pumped quickly, as if it was hooked up to a vacuum. I felt my life draw up toward the sweet sting in my jugular.

Mmmmph mmmmph, Serena grunted.

I grabbed the back of Serena's head and held it tightly as I stood on my tiptoes, thrusting my neck deeper into her mouth, arching my back. I wanted her to drink fast and to get this whole thing over with.

Bubbles filled my brain, and suddenly, dark spots covered my vision, and my body went limp.

"Aaaaaah!" Serena sighed, throwing back her head. She wiped my blood from her lips with the back of her hand and licked her fingertips. "Blood of the babysitter. There is no finer wine in all the world."

I watched hazily as Serena threw her arms up to the sky.

"Brother! You are avenged!" she cried. "Kelly Ferguson, by the Order of the Boogeymen, and in memory of the great Grand Guignol, I hereby pronounce you my slave. You may now kiss my ring."

She held out her slender, magnificent hand. A giant diamond insect sparkled.

"And you may now kiss my butt," I whispered weakly.

Grabbing her hand, I pulled myself up off my knees, slowly rising to look into her eyes.

Serena's smile froze into a peculiar wince. She cleared her throat.

"Your blood. Something is wrong with it," she hissed, touching her trembling lips.

Serena clawed at her neck. Her eight knees wobbled as she tripped over her web. She threw back her head to howl, but it sounded like the honk of a dying goose. Her tongue lashed around like a desperate flag of surrender.

"What have you done?" she asked, staggering forward.

"I am the antidote," I said with a smile.

Her eyes bulged in horror.

"You thought I'd given up? Babysitters never give up!" I shouted.

Serena doubled over. Theo fell from her grip, and I caught him in my arms.

The skin on her face sagged off her skull, and she cried as her human mask flopped onto the ground. The hideous features of a giant spider with two dripping fangs stared down at me.

"Look what you've done to me," she said, grabbing at her skin, trying to hold up her monstrous mask.

The flesh around her hands drooped and fell like

loose gloves to the floor. Her precious jewels skittered from her fingers and neck. She clawed at them, but they scurried out of her grasp into the shadows.

"Look away! Look away!" she shrieked.

I didn't look away. I held Theo against my chest, our hearts thumping together. I felt kind of bad for Serena. All that vanity and talk about beauty and money; it was just a cover-up for an insecure, fragile bug. Her arachnoid mandibles clacked.

Enough chitchat. Get Theo out of here.

I started to climb across the web, but I stopped. Dizzy. Serena had drained so much of my blood I was going to pass out.

No. Not now. Stay awake, Kelly. Keep moving!

Holding Theo, I stumbled on the webbing. Serena raised a lethal limb over me. She was going to kill me. Her spiky, hairy leg rose and then stopped suddenly. It twitched, as if she were a malfunctioning robot. Shaking, Serena's legs curled together, closing around her, like a flower closing its petals for the winter. The hairs on her face and legs grayed and then drained of all color and life. Her spider exoskeleton dried into large flaky scales and wrinkles. Her years of living caught up fast. The Spider Queen withered into a crusty ball and then stopped moving.

The mass of petrified limbs was rigid, silent. It

looked to me like a giant, dead pupa. The kind that a caterpillar bursts out of in the spring.

"Hideous child!" shrieked Professor Gonzalo from the doorway. "The others will not stand for this. They will come for you!"

"Bring it," I mumbled, too weak to argue.

The sniveling Professor and the trolls vanished into the halls of Hargrave Manor.

Holding Theo, I managed to drag myself off the web and onto the chamber floor, beside Liz and Kevin. I was so cold and so tired. I just wanted to sleep forever. And ever.

The moans and wails of Serena's people-puppets trapped in the ballroom were gone. I could hear the astonished cries of my friends, family, and neighbors waking up from a deep, dark spell.

"You broke Serena's hold, newb," Liz said.

"Don't call me 'newb,'" I said as I drifted away into a bright white light, knowing everything was going to be okay for everyone but me. And I was cool with that, even as the world went blank. . . .

Nice knowing ya. In the immortal words of Porky Pig: Th-Th-Th-That's all, folks.

"Kelly? Kelly, *por favor.*"

Something warm touched my lips. Heat radiated down my neck and body. I was pulled from the angelic white light and back to the squalor of Hargrave Manor.

My eyes fluttered open to see Victor's face against mine.

He was kissing me.

Victor is kissing me!

I gasped and jolted up, knocking my forehead against his. Not exactly the smoothest reaction to being kissed, but I was in major shock. One, I think I, like, died. And two, I was being kissed by Victor.

Victor smiled and rubbed his forehead. He had a big smile on his face.

"Get a room you two," Berna groaned. She winked down at me and giggled.

"Seriously, that's very unprofessional," said Curtis.

"I think it'sh romantic," said Cassie, casting her eyes on Curtis.

Mama Vee crossed her arms and raised her eyebrows.

"See what happens when you break Law Number Three?" she said.

I looked at Victor, and my nearly frostbitten cheeks flushed. I realized we were holding hands, our fingers interlaced. Not exactly how I imagined my first kiss would happen, but I would always remember it as the kiss that brought me back to life. I guess some fairy tales are true.

"You guys are okay?" I said.

297

"After you passed out, Wugnot picked the locks on our cuffs, and we escorted everyone outside," said Liz, rubbing her wrists.

Amazed, I looked around. We were outside of Hargrave Manor, surrounded by a mob of family, friends, and neighbors, huddling together in the snow: the once-spellbound police, Tammy, Deanna, Victor's family, and my mom and dad had clear eyes—even if they were totally terrified.

"What about the Professor?" I asked.

Liz grimly shook her head. "Escaped with the trolls."

That made my stomach churn.

"Theo? Theo!" I heard a motherly voice call out. "My baby? Where's my baby?"

Everyone parted and made way for Dawn to rush forward. Her eyes sparkled with life. Mama Vee held Dawn's crying baby in her arms. Dawn scooped up her boy and kissed away the tears on his face.

"My baby boy," she whispered, rocking him back and forth as she pressed his chubby red cheek against her. "My beautiful, little angel. Mommy's here. Mommy's right here."

The little turtle nuzzled his face into his mother's neck. As mother and child were reunited, the storm winds stopped. Gray clouds dissolved into the sparkling starry night. The crowd circled Dawn and her baby with so much love and adoration I thought they were going to start singing "Silent Night."

"Thank you, Kelly," Dawn said to me. Her eyes were shimmering with tears.

I gently rubbed Theo's leg. It was warm and full of life. He was thriving in his mother's arms.

"Just doing my job," I said.

"Kelly?" my mom shouted. "What on Earth are you doing here?"

"Um" was about all I could think to say.

An animal control vehicle, the kind they send to pick up stray dogs, screeched to a stop. A figure stepped from it. She was wearing khaki pants and a crisp white shirt under a snazzy cargo jacket. It was Madame Moon. She held up a badge that made it look like she worked for the city.

"Ladies and gentlemen," Madame Moon barked into a megaphone. "If I could have your attention, please."

The crowd looked to Madame Moon. Stunned. A dozen ambulances, lights flashing, screeched around us. Paramedics rushed out, covering us with blankets, ushering us to the warmth of their vehicles.

"How did we all end up here?" asked Officer Muntz.

While a thousand questions flew, I saw Tammy watching me. The makeup had been washed from her face. She had a knowing look in her eye as she saw me standing with the babysitters.

299

"You have suffered from an outbreak of *Arachnidia narcolepsia*. The sleepwalking snow spider," said Madame Moon as she opened a notebook to a picture of one of Serena's spiders. "The state of Rhode Island recently had an infestation of them, and I'm sorry to say that all of you have been bitten by it. That's right. Reach up, feel your neck. There are probably nasty little bites on your jugular."

My parents felt the tender bites. Victor's mom screamed as she felt hers.

"These are extremely rare spiders with a highly toxic venom that can cause outbreaks of sleepwalking in the victims. Apparently, some concerned citizens saw you all wandering the streets and thought it would be best if you were contained together and kept out of the storm. I would thank them all if I were you. They saved your lives."

Madame Moon gestured to the babysitters and me. She applauded. The other people slowly applauded. They didn't know what to believe. As our neighbors clapped and thanked me and the sitters, Mama Vee gave me a grateful nod.

"Kelly, you saved our lives?" asked my mother, perplexed.

"Guilty," I said with a shrug.

My parents saw the babysitters standing nearby. A look of admiration spread across their faces.

"Well, well," my mother said, a proud smile upon her face. "I guess all that babysitting paid off. Seeing as you had to babysit your father and me."

Hugging my mom and dad, I saw Hank, Liz's father, peering into the darkness beyond the crowd. A flash of red light swept across the shadows, illuminating Liz and Kevin for just a moment. Kevin's silver eyes glistened, looking back at his father. Hank's mouth opened in awe, as if he finally recognized his son in his beastly form.

Another sweep of red light, and Kevin and Liz were gone.

I looked over at Victor, who was holding his family close. Victor was beaming at me, and I guess I was beaming back at him.

40

The next day was a snow day.

No school! Dreams do come true!

The nor'easter had dumped about five feet of glorious, powdery snow across Rhode Island. There was so much snow, all the major highways were closed, which meant my mom and dad had the day off work, too. It was like the world was covered in whipped cream.

Lying in bed, I got a text from Victor:

> Think we can ice-skate on Milton's Pond?

> Heck yes!!!

Even though my body ached, my heart would not let me lie in bed.

"You're not going anywhere until you eat breakfast, young lady," said my mom, standing in my doorway.

"Yes, Mother."

I took down three waffles, six sausage links, four eggs, two glasses of juice, a Pop-Tart, the chicken leftovers we had in the fridge, and a glass of milk. Having my blood drained gave me quite the appetite.

As if I were from an alien planet, my parents watched me as they chewed their toast and sipped their coffee.

"What?" I asked.

My mother shook her head and smoothed her napkin. I had hidden the truth from them for only a month, and it had had terrible consequences. I needed to come clean.

"Do you remember anything about last night?" I asked.

They shook their heads.

"You don't remember inviting someone over for dinner?"

They laughed, shook their heads.

"I think I'd remember that," my dad said.

"You don't remember serving someone you called the most beautiful woman in all the world?" I pressed.

"You mean your mother?" my dad asked.

That made Mom smile. Glad his heart was back in the right place.

I folded my hands and took a deep breath. "Mother. Father. Mom. Dad. I need to tell you something."

I gestured for them to please sit. They did.

"Here's the thing," I said. "I belong to a secret order of babysitters that protects children from the creatures of the night. Last night I took down my second Boogeyperson, Serena the Spider Queen. She sent her spiders to bite you and make you her slaves, which is why the house is such a mess right now. And I am going to continue being a babysitter because Professor Gonzalo, another Boogeyperson, managed to escape. And it's what I'm good at and I love it, and I want you both with me on this journey because one of the things I realized from this whole catastrophe is how much I love and appreciate you guys. But you're going to have to start listening to me and not ground me anymore, because I am about to get into some serious trouble, and the only way I can get through this crazy time of being a teenager, getting good grades, getting into college, and fighting monsters . . . is with your help. I need you guys. Are you with me?"

Toast hung from my father's lips. My mother stared, wide-eyed, as if I had just thrown a bucket of water in her face.

"Maybe we should talk about this later?" I asked

respectfully. "When you've had time to process."

My mother and father nodded.

"'Kay, bye!" I downed the last of my milk and headed for the door, wrapping a fuzzy, autumnal-colored scarf around my neck.

"Bundle up!" my dad said.

"Just did!" I called back, slamming the door.

I grabbed my ice skates from the garage and dusted them off as I sprinted down the block. Rooftops peeked out from under mounds of snow as the blinding frost crunched under my boots.

Red and black sleds shot down the hill beside Milton's Pond. The storm had made the water freeze again. Neighborhood kids were tracing big figure eights across the ice where I had been chased by the Spider Queen, just last night.

As soon as I put on my skates and stepped onto the frozen pond, I realized that my babysitting powers did not include ice-skating. I screamed as I slid across the surface, flailing my arms until I slammed onto my butt.

"K-Ferg in the house!"

Tammy, wrapped in a bedazzled pink scarf and a big fluffy polar bear cap with rhinestones in its eyes, reached down to help me up. Deanna and the Princess Pack were standing at the edge, bored, playing with their phones.

"I haven't been here since I was six," I said.

"Me neither! I forgot how much I suck at skating!" Tammy giggled. "This seemed like such a good idea an hour ago. Now not so much."

"Hold my hand," I said. "We can make it together."

We scuttled across the ice, tripping, holding each other up as we pathetically clomped across the ice.

Swish! Victor skated up to us, spraying us with a wave of snow.

"Not fair," I said, spitting frosty flakes from my mouth. "You're not allowed to be good at this too, Victor. You're from a very warm climate."

"It's just like roller-skating. No?" he said, offering his arm to me like a total gent.

"It's way more slippery than that," I said, taking his arm while holding Tammy's hand. The three of us wobbled across the ice together, laughing.

On the street, waves of snow parted as the babysitter mobile sped into view.

"Ferguson!" Liz shouted.

Playtime was over. I skated to the shore to change back into my boots.

"Tamara, we are scheduled to go to the mall," called Deanna. "My daddy hired a snowplow to get us there. Kooky Kelly can come as long as she doesn't spaz out and wreck the place, and, *Victor*, if you want to come, there's always a seat for you in my dad's Ranger. It's nice and warm."

"I have other plans," Victor said, looking at me.

Tammy shrugged at me. "Wanna come?"

"I do," I said. "But I've got work to do."

Tammy smiled and waved at the babysitter crew.

"Come by later?" Tammy said, elbowing me. "You can tell me all about this." She gestured to Victor and me. "And you need to help me clean up the mess Harriet Hargrave made."

"Deal," I said. "Maybe even sneak in an episode of *A Time of Roses and Cattle*!"

"Deal."

We went our separate ways. Still friends. Just a little different.

I bolted to the van. I looked back and saw Victor standing on the shore, holding his skates by the laces, watching me expectantly.

"C'mon, newb!" I called out.

41

Smoke hissed off the wreckage of our headquarters. The charred, black skeleton of the house jutted up from the mounds of snow. The babysitters stood silently around it, heads bowed.

Curtis's lower lip trembled, and he saluted the ruins while playing a recording of "Taps" on his phone. Wugnot stood at attention with Curtis, his tail rising up to his eye to flick away a few hobgoblin tears. Mama Vee hid her face. She wanted to be strong in front of us, but the sight of her smoldering home was too much for even her to take.

Madame Moon's cold facade melted, and she linked her arms with Vee. "It's just brick and mortar,"

Madame Moon whispered. "The Rhode Island chapter of the Order of the Babysitters has more heart and spirit than can be contained in any building."

Vee smiled.

"You can stay in the Boston headquarters with us," Madame Moon said. "We'll keep you supplied. I'll put in a call to the Chief Childminder in London about helping you rebuild."

"Thank you, Leanne," Vee said.

Wugnot heaved Serena's large skeletal cocoon onto the snow in front of us.

"For starters, you can lock this thing in your basement," said Wugnot.

"Ahh! Kill it with fire!" screamed Curtis.

"Believe me, I tried," said Wugnot. "It's hard as a rock. Best thing we can do is lock it in a cold, dark place and make sure it never falls into the wrong hands."

Madame Moon nodded, pursing her lips at the scabby blob. "I'll have our sitters bag and tag."

Mama Vee looked across the wreckage. "It's never going to be the same again."

An ominous wind shrieked through the snow-covered trees as Madame Moon turned to face me. "You did well last night."

"Doesn't feel like I did," I said quietly. "We lost our headquarters. And we almost lost our president." I looked at Mama Vee. "I'm just glad to have our leader back again."

"From what I heard, they had a leader with them the whole time," Madame Moon said. "One who kept spirits up. Was resourceful. Clever. And made sacrifices above and beyond the call of duty."

I sighed, staring absently at the wreckage.

"You don't have any idea who I'm talking about, do you?" Madame Moon asked.

I shook my head.

"You, Miss Ferguson. It was you."

I raised my chin and saw Madame Moon and Mama Vee looking at me.

"Congratulations, Kelly. You're officially a babysitter," said Madame Moon.

My eyes widened. "I passed?"

"You more than passed, young lady. You shone."

The babysitters cheered. I shouted in glee and did a happy dance. "Yes yes yes yes yes!"

Kevin ambled from the forest. He held wild winter flowers that he had plucked himself. Berries, thorny flowers, weeds, dead branches. Kevin howled apologetically and knelt before Mama Vee and the babysitters, laying his monster bouquet at their feet.

Vee sniffed and petted Kevin's scruffy head.

"You're a beautiful monster, Kevin," Mama Vee said. "I'm glad you're here."

Kevin shook his long, floppy ears and licked Mama Vee on the face, slurping slime all over her cheek. She smiled and wiped the goo off, flicking it back at Kevin.

"Just ask him already," Berna whispered to Cassie.

Cassie took a deep breath. "Curtish. Um. There ish thish guy I like."

"Why you asking me?" Curtis said.

Cassie scowled. Berna gave her an encouraging look. "Becaushe I want your advishe. He doeshn't know I like him."

"Just tell him, Cass," said Curtis. "You're cool."

Cassie swallowed nervously. "Sho, you're shaying, if I like thish guy, I should jusht be shtraighforward and ashk him out?"

"Affirmative."

Cassie was wringing her hands, biting her lip. "Do you want to go out with me?"

"Yep, that's exactly how you should ask him." Curtis nodded.

Cassie stared, dumbfounded. Everyone burst into laughter.

I wanted to laugh with them, but something was digging into the back of my brain, bothering me.

"Professor Gonzalo and the trolls got away," I said.

"Probably went back to his island," said Liz.

"Think there's more kids like Kevin there? Missing kids? Kidnapped kids?" I asked.

Liz nodded. The thought of a place like that made my fingers curl into fists. I had seen the damage the Boogeypeople could do, and it was time I put an end to it.

"We need to go rescue them," I said.

The eyes of the babysitters looked at me. They were my friends, but standing there together with them they felt more like family. A family I knew would face even worse dangers, bigger monsters, and viler Boogeypeople. But if we faced those trials and horrors together, there was nothing we couldn't do.

"Then let's go find that island," I said with steel in my voice. "And bring those kids back."

ACKNOWLEDGMENTS

Wow! What a ride, huh? I don't know about you, but that was intense. Am I right? Could've been a little funnier. Little lighter in parts, no? Well, I was in an intense, heightened state when I wrote *Beasts & Geeks*. My wife had given birth to our son and we suddenly found ourselves in rapturous joy for this beautiful gift of a little person, but I was also pretty scared and frightened. Suddenly Cara and I were responsible for a glowing new life. So this book is all those nerves and fears and fun and craziness of 2017 put into ink and page for your reading pleasure. The glowing light in the dark was always my real-deal, chunky-cheeked chipmunk, who I vowed to protect from the forces of darkness. His incredible mother looked after our boy while I went to fight with monsters and hang out with the cool kids of my imagination. Being a writer is a tough grind, but the girl from East London always keeps my battle-axes sharp and my heart beating.

When I turned in the first draft, Maria Barbo, wonder editor, artist, lighthouse keeper of the flame, sliced over a hundred pages from it. Ouch. Stone-cold! Those were fun pages to write. There was a mummy in the cellar. It was full monster mansion madness. Bye, bye! Slice! But Maria was a hundred percent right. As always. Those pages slowed down the story and were nothing more than whimsy. So you should thank her for sparing you from slogging through a hundred pages that moved like the slow, wheezy mummy all those stupid pages were about. Our editor's assistant, Stephanie Guerdan, has somehow managed to organize all this chaos and keep our stories straight—all while being delightful and kind to a space cadet on a monster planet. Katherine Tegen, Bawss Queen, thank you for your generosity and love for lost, hairy mutants.

Most of you are reading this book right now because of Vivienne To's amazing cover and art. Go on, flick through and check it out; I'll wait. Pretty awesome, right? Vivienne's work brings Kelly's world alive in such a butt-kicking and beautiful way. I can't wait for her to do the animated series.

Alyssa Reuben has been my fairy godmother throughout all these books, occasionally bonking me over the head with her magic wand. Thank you, Alyssa, for being snappy and smart and getting it done. When you dive into the fray, David Boxerbaum, the heavyweight champion of agents, is the man you want at your side. Box can throw down or he can talk about the joys of fatherhood and where the heck to send your kid to preschool.

And finally, and this is cheesy, but I want to acknowledge you, the reader. The best part about writing a book is people reading it and then sharing their feelings about it. I have had a blast hearing what parts scared you silly and what made you laugh. It makes me feel like I'm sitting around a campfire, living my true purpose as a teller of tales. I promise to do my best to empower and inspire you to hope beyond your fears. To be bold and brave for your friends and family and yourselves. You are stronger and bigger and cooler than you could possibly know. So don't be afraid of the dark and don't let the Boogeypeople keep you down.

Until next time, my friends.

THE ADVENTURE CONTINUES . . .

DON'T MISS

A Babysitter's Guide to

MONSTER HUNTING
3

ESCAPE FROM
SUNSHINE ISLAND

Kelly and the babysitters are about to go on a mission to a secret island where the Boogeypeople are transforming missing kids into mutants as part of a nefarious, world-ending plot! And they'll have to do it all while protecting seven-year-old twin sisters with a very big secret.

Will Kelly free the kids, save the day, and still have time to go to the dance? A babysitter's job is never done!